REBELS OF THE HEAVENLY KINGDOM

# Rebels of the

**A NOVEL**

# Heavenly Kingdom

Katherine Paterson

GROUNDWOOD BOOKS
HOUSE OF ANANSI PRESS
TORONTO BERKELEY

Groundwood Books / House of Anansi Press
110 Spadina Avenue, Suite 801, Toronto, Ontario M5V 2K4
or c/o Publishers Group West
1700 Fourth Street, Berkeley, CA 94710

We acknowledge for their financial support of our publishing program the
Government of Canada through the Book Publishing Industry Development
Program (BPIDP).

Library and Archives Canada Cataloguing in Publication
Paterson, Katherine
Rebels of the heavenly kingdom / Katherine Paterson.
Originally published: 1983.
ISBN-13: 978-0-88899-885-9
ISBN-10: 0-88899-885-6
1. China–History–Taiping Rebellion, 1850-1864–Juvenile fiction.
I. Title.
PZ7.P273Re 2008          j813'.54          C2008-902515-6

Calligraphy for dedication by Jeanyee Wong
Design by Michael Solomon
Printed and bound in Canada

For Virginia Buckley
*chien szu wan hsieh*

千思萬謝

a thousand thoughts –
ten thousand thanks

# CONTENTS

# A NOTE TO THE READER

OUT OF MORE THAN four thousand years of Chinese history, this book focuses on three years – 1850 to 1853. The rulers of China at this time were not Han, or native, Chinese. They were Manchu, descendants of northern nomads who conquered China in 1644 and set up the Ching Dynasty, which adopted many of the Confucian ideals of government, becoming in some ways more Chinese than the Chinese. For about one hundred fifty years, the Manchu Empire prospered. But before the middle of the nineteenth century, it had grown weak and corrupt. China was torn from within by natural disasters and peasant uprisings, and threatened from without by foreign powers eager for Chinese raw materials and the chance to sell to such a vast market.

For a while the Manchu resisted those pressures. But after the British won the Opium War of 1840-1842, the Manchu emperor was forced to open

Chinese ports not only for foreign trade and the Christian missionary endeavor but also to permit the importation of opium from British India.

The humiliating defeat of the Manchu army by the long-nose barbarians (as Westerners were called) led to a great wave of Chinese nationalism. Secret anti-Manchu societies flourished, especially in the south of China. Among these were the Taiping Tienkuo — the Heavenly Kingdom of Great Peace. Although fiercely patriotic, the Taiping were greatly influenced by the teachings of Western missionaries. Armed with their own version of Christianity, they embarked upon a holy crusade to save China. This is the story of two people caught up in the Taiping Rebellion

*You should not kill one innocent person or do one unrighteous act, even though it be to acquire an empire.*

—FROM A DECLARATION OF
HUNG HSIU-CH'ÜAN,
THE HEAVENLY KING OF
THE HEAVENLY KINGDOM
OF GREAT PEACE

## CHAPTER ONE
# HUNAN 1850

THE SUN WAS HIGH in the summer heaven, burning Wang Lee's back brick red like the soil into which he dug his hoe. His tunic, now more patch than jacket, was tied around his waist over his equally patched blue trousers. He could feel the warmth of the earth through his straw sandals, and its mild, clean smell filled his nostrils. It was the wrong smell for this time of year. The red earth should have been completely hidden by the bright green of rice in the paddies and the lusher green of cabbage and turnip tops in the tiny square vegetable patches. The air should have hung heavy with the darkly sweet smell of raw manure and wet, rich vegetation. But first had come the deserters from the Imperial banner troops, then the army itself, and finally the bandits, roaming like packs of wild dogs, snatching what scraps had been left by the marauding soldiers. So now the fields stood nearly bare, a great angry wound upon the flesh of the earth.

The boy was digging the last spindly turnips and the single cabbage that had somehow been left to him and his parents. It was all they had to eat, aside from the sickly chicken his mother had managed to conceal under a rice basket. The wretched thing was sure to die soon. He must persuade his mother to kill it first.

The seed rice was behind the fifth brick at the northeast corner of the farmhouse. The fifth brick at the northeast corner... His father kept repeating this as though hammering the knowledge through Wang Lee's fifteen-year-old head.

"No, no," the boy promised. "I won't forget." He shook his head remembering, and his pigtail brushed his hot shoulder. He dropped his hoe and took his kerchief from his waist to tie the hair off his skin. Suddenly the short shadow of his body lengthened at his feet. He lunged for his hoe, but the man behind him was quick, grabbing Wang Lee's queue in one hand and swinging him about with the other.

He was facing a bandit. There was no doubt in Wang Lee's mind, although the man's clothes were too tattered to reveal whether they had ever resembled a uniform. The man had a bristly face and an old kerchief wrapped turbanlike about his head. One eye was red, perhaps diseased, but he carried himself too proudly to be a beggar. Besides, a few paces behind him were two companions to whom he called out in a lordly manner.

"Short Neck! Pinch Face! Now that I've got

this little pig by the tail, what'll we do with him?"

With a great wrench, Wang Lee freed his queue from the man's fist. The man jumped back quickly, drawing a knife from his sash as he did so. His companions pulled their knives as well, and the three men stepped close enough for Wang Lee to smell the stale garlic on their breath and the filth of their unwashed bodies.

"Now calm yourself, Pigboy, or I'll send these two to carve out your mother's liver." Without taking his one good eye off the boy's face, the bandit stooped, picked up the hoe, and tossed it to the one called Pinch Face. "Too bad I can't trust you," he said to the boy, "for now you must dig the rest of those turnips with your fingers." He pointed his knife at the five turnip tops still in the ground. "Dig," he commanded.

Wang Lee squatted before the tiny row — his family's last hedge against hunger. There had been almost enough rain this year, so the turnips loosed themselves from the red soil with little urging. He pitched them into the reed basket with the last cabbage, which he'd dug earlier. He held the basket out to Red Eye. Perhaps if the man saw there was nothing else, the bandits would go on their way. But it was not to be so easy.

"No," said Red Eye. "You carry it. I want to drop by your house and see if there might be a bit of fat to float in my soup tonight."

Dumbly, Wang Lee hoisted the basket to his back and stuck his arms through the bamboo straps. If only the silly chicken would keep quiet. They started for the hut.

When Wang Lee's great-great grandfather purchased the land on which many generations of his family had farmed, he had, in his pride, built a house of bright red brick and thatched it with rice straw. It was only one room, to be sure, and had to be shared by people and pigs — before the pigs were stolen — but it did not belong to a landlord. Neither did it have even the meager protection that the village might have afforded. A lone house was easy prey for thieving.

The boy could see his father at the door watching them come. It did not take long to cross the tiny farm to where the proud peasant stood staring, unbowing and unblinking, at Red Eye's ugly face.

The bandit jerked his head at Pinch Face and Short Neck, who elbowed the farmer aside and stepped over the threshold into the hut. There were the sounds of the table being kicked over and a short cry from his mother, then the feeble *squawk, squawk, squawk* of the chicken, which soon flapped over the threshold only to be snatched up yellow feet first by the waiting Red Eye. His mother came out next, shoved by the two bandits carrying woven rice baskets. She stood for a moment swaying unsteadily on her small, bound feet.

"We're not the first," Pinch Face complained. "There's not much here — quilts — cooking pots — nothing of value."

"Well, get what you can. We'll load the baskets."

Red Eye waved the chicken at them. The poor creature tried to lift its head, managing only a sickly *chirk*.

"The chicken has cholera," his mother said. "It will surely die."

"You are right, Auntie." Red Eye nodded. "It will surely die." All three men guffawed loudly. "On the other hand," Red Eye said, "we could boil the boy. He looks healthy enough."

"No!" cried his mother. "He is my only son. Take the chicken."

"We'll take both," Red Eye said. "And you will fall to your knees and bump your foreheads to the ground that we leave you with your lives and this miserable hut. If anyone asks, remember to tell them that Red Eye was merciful. I'm known for that — my mercy. And next time I come, try to have a pig waiting. I do fancy pork. Now load up," he ordered the others. "And be quick. The boy will be our donkey."

When the baskets were loaded, the only things left were the brick bed built into the wall, the heavy wood table and stools, and the single chest, now empty of padded winter garments and each family member's change of clothing. And the seed rice. The seed rice was still behind the fifth brick in the northeast corner of the wall.

Wang Lee was a little comforted. Maybe his father could sell the furniture, if he could find a way to get it to the market town nine li to the north. His parents were good and pious people. Perhaps the fickle gods would remember the incense at the roadside shrine and the sweet cakes his mother took to the temple almost every new moon.

Red Eye was kicking him. The strip of bamboo that served as a basket pole was slapped to his shoulder. The rope encasing the baskets was hung over the slots at either end of the bamboo. Wang Lee stooped slightly, then began to straighten to lift the baskets. He nearly fell forward on his face. The stupid bandits had not balanced the load.

"Wait," his father commanded, and, under the impatient eyes of the bandits, he carefully repacked both baskets and then tightened the ropes to suit Wang Lee's height. "Now," he said, looking his son full in the face. The farmer's expression did not change, but deep from his unblinking eyes came a blessing and a plea. Wang Lee nodded ever so slightly. No one but his father noticed the movement. It was a promise to his father and to his father's fathers. He would come back to the land bought by their sweat. He would not leave their graves untended or their fields fallow. He did not dare look at his mother.

"Put on your tunic when the sun goes down," she called after him.

He did not look back at the little house or the single persimmon tree growing out of the beaten earth, or at his parents. Behind him he could hear his mother weeping. It was not her funeral cry, but a quiet sobbing he had not heard before. It moved him more than wailing.

He was a strong boy and used to heavy loads, and

he began this strange journey at the careful trot of a peasant accustomed to hurrying to market without damaging his wares. His father's gift of a perfectly balanced load was a blessing, and the bandits had to push to keep up his pace.

Within three hundred steps, he had left the land worked by his ancestors for more generations than could be remembered. Three hundred more and he had passed the rocky hillside that held their whitened bones. He was still running strong, his shadow barely lengthened, before he had gone farther from his people than he had ever traveled in his life. They were headed west, though no one spoke of destination. Far to his back, the mountains marked the limit to the plains. And ahead, though he could barely see it, rose the height of Heng Mountain. At first the farmlands through which he ran were red and bare like his own. But before dusk, they entered a land where soldiers had not come, where the second rice had been harvested and the straw left carelessly to dry in the fields, where the first shoots of the third rice were well above the waters of the beds, nearly ready for transplanting.

From time to time, the bandits would make him stop so they could rest, settled on their haunches like angry toads. "Your pigboy has crow wings," Pinch Face complained. He had torn a lotus leaf out of a pond and was using it for a fan, holding his tunic out from his body and fanning the sweaty chest underneath. His companions were too short of breath to reply.

But Wang Lee seemed to draw new breath from the lush greenness as he ran on the narrow paths of the paddies, skirting the little hills that rose abruptly before them — the hills that some said were the burial places of the ancients, inhabited by ghosts.

By dusk he was long past tiredness. He was running in a dream. Perhaps he could have run on forever until he met the great tiger at the western edge of the earth. The path beneath his feet was hardly visible, and the sun had fallen over the side of the world. This made him begin to think of food and rest and shelter for the night.

"My belly clings to my backbone," muttered Pinch Face from behind him.

"Aieee," Short Neck wailed. "I'll soon be too exhausted to eat."

In the distance the smoke of a farming village rose up against the dark sky. "There's a place," Short Neck said. "A nice cool brick bed to sleep on. Rice all cooked. A little soup…"

"Stupid son of a turtle." Red Eye spat noisily into the irrigation canal beside the path. "You fall asleep on that nice cool bed and you'll find your skull furrowed like a cabbage patch. Those rascals would show more tenderness butchering a hog. As for me, I'd rather dare the dull knives of ghosts. This way, Pigboy," he commanded, herding the little group toward the shadow of a nearby hill.

The boy knew at once that the hill contained a temple, for it was covered with trees. Most hills were stripped bare. Even in hard times, the trees of the temple groves were sacred, and anyone who didn't agree would have to answer to a burly priest. If there was a temple, perhaps there would be no ghosts. Perhaps. But he could feel a chill go through his bare back as soon as they left the path beside the paddy and headed up the small winding way under the pine trees. Just to be safe, he worked up saliva in his dry mouth, spit three times, and recited an incantation against ghosts and demons.

He heard a laugh behind him, and then the sound of more spitting. "For luck," Short Neck explained.

"Yes, yes, for luck," Pinch Face echoed.

It was a low hill, less than four hundred steps to the flat summit where a small wooden building stood with a threshold hardly high enough to keep out even the most timid demon. Red Eye shouted out a greeting that sounded more like a threat, but there was no reply except the raucous complaint of a flock of crows who fluttered up from the trees, circled the hill, and then, cawing in annoyance, settled down once more for the night.

Red Eye was inspecting the small temple and courtyard as best he could in the moonlight. "There is a well," he said, "and there is brush under the trees." He sent the two men to gather fuel. "You can deal with the bird," he said to Wang Lee. "Wring its neck."

The boy took off the top of the front basket. "The chicken is dead," he said, the first words since morning scratching his dry throat.

"Obliging bird."

The boy thought the bandit did not understand. "It was sick," he explained. "It had cholera. You do not eat a sick bird after it dies."

"Doesn't it squawk if you try eating it alive?"

The boy shrugged. He knew he would eat some if they allowed it. He was too hungry to be careful.

Red Eye ordered him to draw water from the courtyard well. He could hear it slopping over the sides of the bucket as he wound the rope. His throat almost closed with thirst. Red Eye called the others to come. Wang Lee watched as all three men drank deeply and then poured water over their heads. They handed him back the empty bucket. He hesitated. They were still squeezing the water from their wet garments, laughing and slapping their great feet on the paving stones of the courtyard. Furtively, he dropped the bucket down once more into the darkness and hauled it back as quickly as he could. When it got to the top, he thrust his head all the way into the water, only to be jerked back by the pigtail.

"Ya! Ya!" Red Eye shook a finger at him as he held the queue tightly in the other hand. "Not until your elders are satisfied." Short Neck grabbed the bucket and sloshed the water once more over his head. At least the boy's shaven forehead was cool and there was a taste of wetness on his parched lips. He licked them while he drew more water for the wasteful bandits, until at last they tired of their game and set their minds once more on gathering dry grass and brush for the fire. Using Wang Lee's mother's flint and iron, Red Eye started a healthy flame. Then he yelled for Wang Lee to fill the cooking pot with water and bring it to the fire to boil.

The bandits watched carefully, stretched out like lazy dogs on the pavement of the courtyard, as Wang Lee plunged the already stiff chicken into the bubbling water to loosen the feathers and then plucked it expertly. At home every feather would have been saved for a quilt, but here he let them fall wasted to the stones. The naked bird was returned to the pot, along with torn cabbage leaves and two of his father's turnips. He wiped each one carefully on the back of his left hand. Several days later he could still smell the odor of his father's land on his skin and feel comforted by it.

"What's taking so long?" Pinch Face asked. "I'll die of old age if I don't die of starvation first."

The boy did not bother to answer. If they wanted to eat a raw chicken stiff with death before it reached the pot, that was their affair.

A bit of yellow fat was floating to the top of the water. Red Eye stood up and came to the fire. He squatted beside it, pulling out a small cloth purse from somewhere inside his tatters. The boy was puzzled. Why should the bandit be taking his money out? But the treasure was not money. It was salt, precious as money, which Red Eye took from the purse — a pinch between his dirty thumb and forefinger and carefully dropped into the soup. He settled back on his haunches, watching the bubbles with his bad eye closed. "Sell or keep?" he asked the fire.

The boy thought he meant the meal.

The bandit went on. "He's strong and useful, but he'll need feeding and watering like a buffalo calf." Red Eye sniffed. "Who would pay me what he's worth?"

"What about a long-nose barbarian?" said Short Neck. "They can hardly walk for the silver in their pockets, and they come from mountains made of gold."

"The long-noses don't buy peasants — only emperors and sometimes an official or general," Red Eye replied. The other two laughed derisively. "Manchu meat, being so tenderly cared for, is quite a delicacy compared to that of us Han Chinese."

"They do eat human flesh, you know," said Pinch Face. "Those Europeans."

"You lie!" Short Neck sat straight up in his surprise.

"I swear. It is a religious ceremony with them. They eat flesh once a week. With much chanting and carrying on."

"Chinese or barbarian?"

"Who knows? It's all cut up into tiny pieces and the blood squeezed out. They drink the blood separately."

"No!"

"My cousin told me. During the last famine, he went to the courtyard of a long-nose temple in Canton where they were giving away food. And after they gave him a little soup, they made him go into the temple. That's where he saw it."

Short Neck slapped his knee in delight. "Wah! That would give you a fright."

"Fright? He ran so fast out of there it took his pigtail a week to catch up with his nose."

All three men slapped themselves and roared with pleasure.

"I saw a long-nose once," Red Eye bragged.

"You didn't."

"Indeed I did. His eyes were blue as rice mold, and his hair as red as a poisonous toadstool."

"Ahhhhh," his companions sighed.

"And his nose?" Pinch Face asked.

"What a nose! Who could believe it? It began in the very center of his forehead, higher than his hideous blue eyes, and ended in a terrible hook over his mouth." Red Eye's large hand swept out from his forehead to his lips to indicate the monstrous proportions of such an appendage.

"Ahhh," the men sighed again, longing to see for themselves such a marvelous freak of nature.

"It was a few winters ago," Red Eye said. "I was temporarily a member of the emperor's troops at the time. We had been sent down south to smash a nest of rebels." He took time to turn his head and spit. Wang Lee could not tell whether this was at the Manchu emperor or the rebels. "They claimed to be children of the gods, but they fought like sons of the devil," the bandit continued. "I decided to keep my queue and the head attached to it a bit longer, so I wandered away from the army over toward Canton. That's where I saw the long-nose." He sniffed, no longer interested in his own tale. "Hey you, son of a turtle, what about our soup?"

The boy jerked to attention. He had been listening to the bandit's story and had forgotten to feed the fire, which was almost out. He hastened to add more grass, using up his meager supply. "The fire needs more fuel," he said.

"Then get it." Red Eye waved him away. "But don't get smart, or I'll go back and remove your father's ears."

In the dark, away from the shadowy light of the small fire, the boy scrabbled about on his hands and knees, looking for something that would burn. Dry grass blazed up brightly but burned too quickly, and moss smoldered. If only he had a bit of hard dung or dry wood. He got up and went into the tiny temple. It was too black inside to see, but he moved instinctively toward the opposite wall. The wooden railing guarding the idols remained, old and rotten. He grasped with both hands to locate it, and then still in the blind darkness, he charged it with his right foot. It splintered with a crash against the stone floor. He tore the broken piece from the wall.

The bandits had come running to the doorway. Wang Lee, now more accustomed to the blackness, could make out the whites of their wide eyes.

"We needed fuel," he said, dragging the railing past them into the courtyard. They stepped back. He held one end of the railing with his left hand and smashed again and again with his right foot to break it into short lengths. Then he put a couple of these carefully onto the fire.

"Sell him," Red Eye was saying almost to himself. "He has no more respect for the gods than a long-nose."

The boy wondered if the bandit might be a little afraid of him. It was not an unpleasant idea.

The chicken was stringy and the soup thin, but the meal satisfied their gnawing bellies. After the bandits had filled their bowls, the boy had his share too. They had not stopped him. He wondered idly if the tainted meat might kill them all, but he fell into a dreamless sleep and awakened the next morning stiff for having slept on stones with no quilt but as healthy as ever.

And hungry. He got the flint and iron — how was his mother managing without them? — and started the fire. There was plenty of water and now plenty of fuel and soup left from the night before. His captors were still snoring. He could run away. Would they follow him? Would they carry out their threats against his parents? They knew where his home was. He shivered.

As he stirred the soup, he tried to comfort himself. He had been kidnapped, yes, but things could be worse. His captors could have been soldiers. As it was, they were simply stupid and dishonorable rascals. At home, even if he could manage to return there without risk to himself or his parents, there was no food, no work. His parents were better off without him to feed. He would stay with his captors as long as he had to. Perhaps he could see something of the world. He imagined for a moment what it would look like. Perhaps he could make a fortune in a distant city. Then how glad his parents would be to see him return in a sedan chair borne by four chair bearers. He would be dressed in silks like an official, and he would be carrying thousands of taels of silver in his purse. And in his head he would be carrying the greatest treasure of all — he would be able to read and write. Once in the market town, he had seen such a rich scholar. Often he had dreamed of him.

There was a stand of bamboo growing at the back of the deserted temple. He took his mother's knife from the basket and dug down to find a tender shoot to add to the soup. He also found a few black-eared tree mushrooms and marveled that the peasants of this district were so wealthy that they would leave such delicacies unharvested.

As the soup bubbled merrily, he drew water from the well and washed his whole body. Only the back of his left hand remained unwashed. He wanted the smell of his father's field to stay there where he had wiped it with the turnip, as a sign that he would return and comfort them in their old age. He was their only son. Three older sisters were long married and now belonged to their husbands' families. He was the last of his. Otherwise his father would have sent him to school. A farmer with more than one son could afford to allow one of them to learn to read and write. If the boy was clever enough, he could take the Imperial examinations, and if he passed, he might become a person of power and authority, perhaps even of wealth. But his unlucky father had only one son who must remain a farmer and tend the land of his ancestors.

But now, strangely, fate had intervened. He had been snatched unwillingly from home, but somehow this did not seem as dreadful as it had yesterday. He was going to see the world, and with his mother's chicken, he had more than a day's worth of food. There was nothing like a full stomach to cheer the heart.

## CHAPTER TWO
# To Kweilin

THERE WAS A QUARREL among the bandits after breakfast. They were lounging on the warm stones of the courtyard, their bellies filled, so it was a lazy argument about what to do next.

"We agreed from the beginning to go south," Red Eye was saying with a belch. "We spent last winter in the north. You haven't forgotten?"

"They say the south is crawling with troops. More soldiers in Canton than maggots on a corpse," Pinch Face said. "We've lost our taste for forced marches with no pay, eh, Short Neck?"

Short Neck gave no reply. He was stretched out flat on his back, his mouth slightly open. A fly was buzzing about his lips, and whenever it lit, he twitched his mouth to make it go away. Otherwise he did not move.

Red Eye propped himself up on an elbow. When he saw that Short Neck was asleep, he picked up a pebble and threw it at the man's face. It bounced off his cheek, causing the bandit to sit up abruptly, blinking wildly.

"You'll lose what neck you've got if you're not more careful where you fall asleep," Red Eye said. "Pinch Face here says you've lost your appetite for army life."

Short Neck could only nod, still blinking in the bright sun.

"Shall we head for the river then? And from there southwest into the mountains where a respectable Chinese bandit can find food and companionship and never need fear the running dogs of the Manchu emperor?"

The other two were quick to agree. The idea of riding a riverboat seemed far more pleasant than trotting behind Red Eye's pigboy. But even with the decision made, they dawdled about until the sun was indicating noon before they began their descent of the hill. And it was dusk before they reached the river.

When they came at last to the water, there was not a boat in sight. The bandits, however, preferred sitting on their haunches on the riverbank to walking further. Wang Lee had brought along pieces of the altar railing, so by gathering some dry grass he could quickly build a fire. He drew a potful of water from the river, strained out the floating garbage, and then boiled it with some of the remaining cabbage leaves and the chicken bones he'd managed to save. The greedy bandits had eaten all the meat and the turnips.

Red Eye added his pinch of salt. It was a watery soup at best, but hot. When they had eaten, Red Eye sent the two bandits off to steal vegetables from a nearby field. By the time they returned with their basket half-full of turnips and long-leafed cabbage, they spotted the dark shape of a boat coming slowly up the river. As it drew closer, Wang Lee could see that it was being towed. The rope from the bow was drawn over the shoulder of a man who was bent nearly double, his whole body straining forward as he moved turtlelike up the path beside the water.

Red Eye went to meet him. The others were too far away to hear the conversation, but the man did not stop his painful forward progress. He simply allowed Red Eye to fall into step beside him. By the time they got to where Wang Lee and the two bandits waited, the contract had been made — a free ride as far as the next market town "with our pigboy doing the pulling."

Pinch Face and Short Neck jumped down to the low deck. Red Eye was about to follow when he stopped. "Wait," he said. "Someone must stay awake to herd our little pig, lest he go astray in the darkness." So that night the three bandits took turns walking beside the boy as he pulled.

Wang Lee put on his tunic and then took the rope from the old boatman, whose sparse gray hair, few yellowed teeth, and bone-thin frame made it look as though he were being held together by the wide cotton girdle bound about his waist. Wang Lee put the rope over his own strong shoulder and stepped forward. Nothing happened. The boat refused to follow. He spit at the river, hoisted the rope more firmly to his shoulder, and strained ahead with all his might. To his annoyance, all the men were staring at him. The old boatman was laughing out loud. Wang Lee clenched his teeth and tensed his muscles. The effort sent a rivulet of pain shooting up the left side of his forehead and across his skull, but he could not give in to it, not with the old man laughing.

The boat began to move at last, and when it did, the boy almost fell to his knees, but he caught himself and pushed ahead. Slowly, slowly in the moonlight, like a worm or an ant bearing a great grain of rice, his arms, his shoulders, and the back of his strong young legs stretched to the screaming point, while the boatman, sitting on his haunches, cackled with glee and called up to him from the deck that he must not go so fast. "Why, at such a speed you will leave the lazy moon behind, and then how will we see to travel?"

The sweat filled Wang Lee's eyes, but he did not dare stop to retie his kerchief about his forehead. One straw-sandaled foot shoved past the other, on and on through the night, until at last the half-moon left the sky and there was not enough light to see his toes. The boatman cried out that he must stop — he would not have the fool pig ramming his boat in the dark. Without apparent effort, he lifted the stone anchor and pitched it overboard, then leapt to the bank as nimbly as a young goat and took the rope from Wang Lee's burning shoulder.

"Not so strong as you thought, eh?" and cackling again, the old man half shoved the boy to the deck, taking care, however, that Wang Lee did not fall into the crack between boat and bank.

With every muscle, every sinew of his body stitched into a tight pattern of pain, Wang Lee could not loose himself to true sleep. But bound in a hot stupor of exhaustion, he knew nothing outside his own body until he was kicked. The sun was already high. He thought at first he would not be able to unfold himself to sit up, much less to stand, but a few more well-placed kicks and he was struggling to his feet. The boatman had a clay stove burning on the deck, and when he had finished boiling his own gruel, he allowed Wang Lee to put on water from the river and boil a vegetable soup for the bandits.

The bandits let him have a bowl of soup but then ordered him to the towpath once more. This time he walked alone. The bandits seemed to know that he had no strength to run. The rope might as well have been tied around his body. When at last they came upon the market town, the bandits tried to persuade the boatman to take them further, but he was unwilling, and there were too many people around for them to try to force his help. They wandered down the dock until they found another boatman headed their direction who agreed to carry them upstream with the promise of a towing in exchange for passage.

Day blurred into succeeding day, broken only by the short periods of blackness when Wang Lee was allowed to stop and curl his burning flesh against the wooden deck boards. At some point, he would never remember when, the river (or was it some other river?) wound upward into the mountains, and they were beyond Hunan and in the province of Kwangsi. They had changed boats two or three times, but to Wang Lee it was the same rope, the same rocky path, the same deck boards. From time to time there was a favorable wind, and he would be shoved on board to lie curled on the deck while the sail carried them easily against the current, covering as many li in an hour as he could manage in a day of towing. Once they sailed for two whole days. And by the end of the second, he had gathered enough strength to pull himself over to the side of the boat and watch the sail. It seemed to him like the wing of a mighty bird carrying them past the mountains of this world to the magic mountain that stands at the end of the world.

Cut through the heart of the mountains was a gift of the gods, an ancient canal that took them at last to a river whose water flowed to the south. Wang Lee would not have to tow any longer. He fell upon the deck and slept. When he opened his eyes, he thought he was dead. For surely what he saw was the end of the world — mountains he could never have imagined rising abruptly from the green plain like giant pockmarked gods whose heads were crowned with clouds. But before the day was over, they had floated into a mortal city and made their way to an inn that bore no resemblance to Paradise.

Wang Lee was the son of a farmer and used to the smell of animals and fresh manure, but nothing had prepared him for the putrid odor of a city inn. He was grateful when the innkeeper sent them to sleep on the cobblestones of the courtyard. Red Eye sold a piece of bedding and bought cheap wine and a foul-tasting soup. The bandits, deluded by the wine, did not seem to notice the quality of the soup. But Wang Lee, sitting with his back against the court-yard wall, had no wine. And hungry as he was, he could hardly put his mouth to the bowl without gagging.

"Fah!" said a voice beside him. "This isn't soup. It's turtle waste."

The words were rough as a peasant's, but the tone was almost elegant. Wang Lee turned to stare at the speaker. He was dressed in the blue clothes and broad straw rain hat of a peasant, and he was using the lan-guage of a peasant, but something didn't match. The boy took a long, noisy sip from his noxious bowl. Now the stranger was looking straight at him.

"Your belly must be chopped from rock."

Wang Lee shrugged. "They do call me Pigboy."

The man laughed, recognizing his feeble joke. "Come, little brother," he said, standing and pour-ing his own soup on the stones. "Let's find some-thing fit for men to eat."

When Wang Lee hesitated, the man said, "I will pay." Still Wang Lee dared not get up. He could feel

Red Eye's threatening gaze even without looking that way. Red Eye rose to his feet and strode over.

"What business do you have with my boy?" he asked, leaning so close to the stranger that he nearly hit the man's hat brim. The bandit had drunk enough to sound cruel but not enough to sound stupid.

The man was several inches shorter than Red Eye. He did not back off but returned the bandit's stare. "I was offering to buy the boy something fit to eat. It is clear you feed him poorly."

"He eats as well as I do, though it's no business of yours." At first Wang Lee thought Red Eye might strike the man, but the bandit stopped himself in midair and changed course. "I was thinking of selling the boy," he said smoothly. "I can't afford to keep him. He eats far too much, if the truth be known, and is lazy as a sow in the sun." He smirked. "Your clothes may be of blue cloth, but I hear in your voice that you are a man of some position. A clever master like yourself might get a fair day's work out of such a one."

"So you'd part with him cheap?"

"Ah, if only I could and be done with it." Red Eye wiped his mouth and then his runny eye on his sleeve. "I paid far too much for him, and I must at least get that back." His voice dropped. "I had to borrow the money...."

"From your old blind mother, of course."

"If only it were so simple." Red Eye sighed. "It was a moneylender who would sell his own blind mother to make a single copper."

"The lad is skinny and looks ill used. I will give you twenty silver taels for him."

"Oh, my young master. If only I could oblige you. I paid thirty for him a month ago, and he has done nothing but eat since."

"Twenty and not a copper more."

The young gentleman shrugged and started away. Wang Lee's heart sank. The man had reached the gate before Red Eye called out, "Twenty-five, but you rob me!"

The gentleman pretended not to hear.

"Twenty-two, you bandit!"

Still the man didn't turn or even slow his walk.

"Twenty-one, but you must reimburse me for his boat fare from Hunan."

To Wang Lee's joy, the gentleman turned. "Twenty plus his lodging for tonight."

"But the boat fare!"

"Twenty plus the lodging." The gentleman was already counting out the silver and copper from his purse. The sight of actual money was too much for the bandit.

"Curse you for being a thief," Red Eye said, reaching out his hand.

"Come," the gentleman said to Wang Lee. "The sooner we get out of this pesthole, the better."

# CHAPTER THREE
## THE YOUNG MASTER

IT WAS A MIRACLE. The gods had heard his mother's prayers. Wang Lee followed his new master out of the stinking courtyard down the dark, narrow streets of the city. He had no idea where the gentleman was going, but it didn't matter. Anywhere this kind young man went would be better than where he had been this past month.

They walked rapidly away from the inn, the new master in the lead, Wang Lee a step or two behind, eager to show respect and gratitude to his unexpected savior. The gentleman was only an inch or two taller than himself, but seemed slightly stockier. His walk invited the same questions as the grace of his voice. Wang Lee decided that the man must be a southerner. He had heard that these southern gentlemen were strange creatures. This fellow had probably traveled all over China. He'd seen the Forbidden City in Peking and the island full of long-noses in Canton. You could tell by the way he walked that he had seen the world. Undoubtedly he could read and write. He could probably recite the entire Classics of Confucius if asked. You could tell by the straight line of his back what a wonderful man he was.

Suddenly the gentleman turned into a small alleyway. Wang Lee nearly tripped on his own sandals in his eagerness not to be left behind. At a massive wooden gate, the gentleman stopped, gave a few short raps, and waited. The gate swung inward, and the man went over the threshold and nodded at Wang Lee to follow.

The young boy who had opened the gate closed it and led them across a small courtyard toward a house that looked in the moonlight to be twice the size of Wang Lee's father's house. Inside there seemed to be a number of people gathered about a table, though it took his eyes a minute to adjust to the smoky light that came from a wick swimming in a dish of peanut oil at the center of the table.

No one spoke as they came across the threshold. "It is all right, my brothers," the young master said. "The boy is a slave brought here from Hunan by robbers. They sold him cheaply, so they must have kidnapped him and abused him. Please be kind to him."

A tall man rose from his stool. "Have you eaten yet, little brother?" he asked. Wang Lee started to reply politely that he had, but the young master interrupted. "There was nothing to eat at that inn but pig swill. We would both be grateful for something."

A place was made at the table for the two of them, and stools were set. Wang Lee hesitated. He was, after all, a slave, but his master nudged him forward and then sat down beside him. The gentleman removed the straw hat from his head and handed it to the boy who had brought them in. The boy hung the hat on a peg and disappeared into another room, coming back in a minute to give them warm damp towels with which to wipe their hands and faces. It was not until that moment that Wang Lee realized that his master's head was not shaved. Moreover, the narrow pigtail that had hung down his back had disappeared with the straw rain hat, and the gentleman had shaken a hatful of long, glossy black hair down upon his shoulders.

The unshaved head could only mean that Wang Lee's savior was a rebel — a member of one of the many secret societies bent on overthrowing the Manchu emperor. But the false pigtail on the hat, the great amount of thick hair that had been concealed in the hat… Wang Lee broke into a sweat. He began rewiping his face in agitation. So *that* was why this gentleman had such a strange elegant voice, why his walk had seemed peculiar. Wang Lee had been tricked!

What kind of a person could she be? Running about pretending to be a man. She wasn't a lady. A lady would have had proper bound feet. Hers were as large as a man's. Even his peasant mother had bound feet. Not so small as a lady's, of course, but still bound, still dainty. While this brazen creature...

She was laughing now at his embarrassment. "See, brothers," she said to the others. "You don't have to fear for me. The boy never suspected."

"You—you are a woman!" Wang Lee stammered. Now everyone was laughing. "And—and a traitor!" The laughter stopped abruptly.

She leaned toward him, her arms on the table. "Not a traitor," she said, all the music gone from her voice. "We are true Chinese. Our leader has been given the Mandate of Heaven. It is the Manchu devil who calls himself our emperor who is the false king."

Just then the serving boy put steaming bowls of rice before Wang Lee and the young woman, and then a dish of pork and vegetables for them to share.

"Eat, little brother," she said gently. "Slowly, though, for I fear you have not eaten properly for a long time."

He was confused. These kind people, this strange woman speaking of the emperor just as the bandits had. He nodded to show her he understood, and then lifted the sweet-smelling rice bowl in his left hand and the chopsticks in his right. Ah, what an odor. He took a tiny bite and chewed carefully. Without meaning to, he sighed. What kind of people would feed a slave just as they fed the master — the mistress?

She smiled. "That's right," she said. "Very slowly. It would not do if our good food made you ill." He ate as slowly as he could, savoring each delicious bite. Even the food at his father's table in time of plenty had not tasted so fine. From time to time, with her encouragement, he dipped his chopsticks into the dish and took more of the pork-flavored vegetables. The garlic and ginger warmed and delighted his mouth. The serving boy brought them salty pickles and tea, and when Wang Lee had nearly finished, she spoke again. "When you are through, you are free to go."

"Go?"

"You may return to your home. We will not keep you here against your will."

He was more confused than ever. "But you bought me," he said.

"We do not keep slaves," she said. "Man or woman or child. If we buy one, it is simply to buy freedom for a child of Heaven."

He did not trust her. "Who are you that you should be so merciful to someone like me?" he asked politely.

"We cannot answer that question," the tall man said. "We are not traitors, but many will call us that. If we tell you our secrets, only to have you go forth from us, we put many lives in danger."

"It would be better," the young woman went on, "for you simply to remember that we are your brothers and sisters, that we are merciful because Heaven commands mercy." She took out her small purse and put three silver pieces beside him on the table. "For your journey," she said.

He shook his head. He could not take money. It

would shame him to do so. "No," he said. "No. I could never repay…"

She took his hand — hers was nearly as large as his — and pressed the money into it. "You may call it a bribe," she said. "We pay you never to speak of this night."

"I would never betray you." He was angry to think she feared he might.

But she kept her hand closed around his. "You will never reach home otherwise," she said softly. "Our lives are in the hands of Heaven. We have not met by accident. Heaven will give you a chance to repay."

He bowed as he got up from the table, the money in his hand. The young woman and her companions rose and offered him a formal good-bye — as though he had been a gentleman visitor at their table. He backed out, bowing, and then followed the serving boy to the large wooden gate.

Not in all the days since he had been kidnapped had Wang Lee felt more alone. He stood blinking in the darkness, barely able to see the gate that had closed behind him, knowing that within were the strange young woman who had saved him and her kind companions. If he left now when it was dark, he would never find the house again. He should have asked for lodging for the night. He was so tired. They would not have thrown him out. He could not make himself go out of the alley into the street. He didn't know whether to turn left or right. He didn't know the way to the river, and all the gates of the city would be closed. His silver pieces were likely to be stolen in these narrow streets. No, he couldn't go now. He went back down the alley to the gate, curled himself against the threshold, and fell asleep.

Someone was picking him up. He was dimly aware of what was happening and started to struggle free until he realized that he was being carried through the gateway. He gave way and allowed himself to be taken in, laid on a wooden bed, and covered with a quilt.

"Poor little brother," the young woman said, for she was one of the two who had carried him in. "Didn't I say he would join us?" she asked.

And so it was decided. For although Wang Lee could have sat up and denied it, he did not. Whether it was because he was too tired or too grateful or too curious, he never really knew.

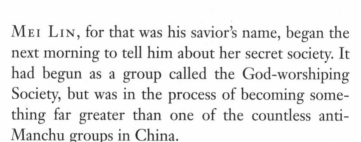

## CHAPTER FOUR
# THE HEAVENLY KINGDOM OF GREAT PEACE

MEI LIN, for that was his savior's name, began the next morning to tell him about her secret society. It had begun as a group called the God-worshiping Society, but was in the process of becoming something far greater than one of the countless anti-Manchu groups in China.

"Our leader, whose name is Hung Hsiu-ch'üan, bore in his youth the ambition to be a scholar. Although he was only the son of a poor farmer, he devoted his life to study, and when the Manchu emperor proclaimed the Imperial examinations, he was an applicant. But being poor, he lacked money to give gifts to the corrupt Manchu examiners, so despite his repeated efforts, he did not obtain even the lowest degree.

"After the third attempt, not knowing even then that the Hand of Heaven is at work in all things, he fell into despair so deep that he became ill. He lay in bed for forty days, unable to communicate even with his family. But while his body lay close to death, his spirit ascended to Heaven. There he saw an old man with a beard of gold wearing a robe of ebony. This Venerable One called him the Tien Wang — the Heavenly King — and gave him a sword and commanded him to slay the demons. Then the Venerable summoned the teacher Confucius. The scholar who has been the source of all our learning for these two thousand years was scorned and whipped like a naughty schoolboy. Our leader was shocked and wondered how this could be, for he himself honored Confucius above all other men. And it was explained to him that Confucius had failed to include in all his writings the truth about the Heavenly Kingdom of Great Peace. But the Venerable in His mercy knew that Confucius was only ignorant, not evil, and so He allowed him to stay in Heaven."

Wang Lee's head was exploding. He could read and write exactly one character, his own family name, Wang. But even he, an ignorant son of an illiterate farmer, knew that Confucius was to be honored like a god. What nonsense had he fallen into?

"Now when Hung recovered from his illness, he remembered the vision clearly, but he did not understand its meaning."

Small wonder, thought Wang Lee.

"For six more years he studied, and once more he journeyed to Canton to take the Imperial examinations. That was the last time. He knew when his name did not appear upon the list, that Heaven had given him a greater honor than that of becoming an Imperial scholar. He knew the day would come when he would examine the scholars of the empire." She waited as though expecting Wang Lee to make some comment. What did she want him to say?

"Good," he said. She was still waiting. "Uh—very good."

"It was at that time," she continued without indicating whether or not his answer had satisfied her, "that Heaven revealed to him the meaning of his earlier vision."

Wang Lee's belly was full and his eyes heavy. A fly was buzzing lazily about his nose. He blew gently to disturb it, remembering as he did so Short Neck asleep in the temple courtyard. He wondered where they were — not that he cared — not that they had ever been the least bit kind to him. But even so, there had been no lectures to make his head ache.

"Are you listening?" she asked sharply, as though reading characters written on his forehead.

He jerked to attention. "Yes, yes," he said. "The meaning of — of your leader's vision."

"*Our* leader's vision," she corrected. "The meaning was found first in a pamphlet that the Heavenly King had received some years before from a long-nose foreigner. In reading it, our leader learned that the Venerable with the golden beard was none other than the Supreme Lord, the High God of all the world, who, as he had revealed in the vision, had chosen our leader to be the Heavenly King on earth."

She was waiting again.

"Remarkable," the boy suggested.

This time she nodded.

"Truly remarkable!" he said, happy to be on the right path.

"Now there are many things about the Heavenly Kingdom that you must learn." Wang Lee's head tightened. "But you cannot learn them all in one day." What relief. "Today we will only settle the matter of a name for you."

"I have a name," he said. "I told you earlier. It is Wang. Wang Lee."

"That was your name when you were still in ignorance," she said, not unkindly. "Now you understand. Wang means king."

"It is also my name," he said. "I have not always been a slave. My father owns land in Hunan, as did his father and his father's father before him. Our family is very old in our district."

She was shaking her head.

"You do not believe me." He wanted her to believe him, to be impressed. "I was kidnapped by those bandits. Right off my father's land I was taken."

"Of course I believe you, little brother. But it doesn't matter. In the Heavenly Kingdom, only those that the High God, the Heavenly Father, calls to be king can bear the name of Wang. No others are permitted this name. We must respect this." She smiled, trying to reconcile him to the loss of his name. "You may have the name of Huang or Kuang, if you like."

"But Wang is very easy to write," he said miserably.

"Kuang is almost as easy," she said.

"I do not know Kuang. It is not my father's name."

"Come," she said. "You are a clever boy. Don't be upset."

"I did not know you would take away my name."

"But we will give you a new name. Do not cling to your old life with its old name."

"It is the only word I can write," he said finally, his head down.

"Ah," she said. "Then it is hard to give it up. What if I teach you to write another?"

"You're nothing but a woman."

She had been leaning toward him over the table, but at this she sat up straight. "In the Heavenly Kingdom there is no difference between male and female. Before the High God, all are equal. We are all given learning. We may all own land. And" — her voice dropped to a whisper — "should the demons attack, we shall all fight."

He was liking the Heavenly Kingdom less and less with every passing moment. To lose his name. To be taught by a woman whose feet were large and ugly. To hint at fighting. "I think," he said slowly, "I should like to go home after all."

Her eyes shone dark from her sunburned face. "It is too late to speak of leaving now. Last night you were free to leave. Today you know who we are. We cannot let you go." Her voice was very quiet, but he felt a threat in the words nevertheless.

As little as he wanted to stay, he wanted less to die.

"Very well then." She went on as if the last words had not been said, as though she were still the kind elder sister who had rescued him and wanted only the best for him. "If Huang or Kuang do not suit you, what name do you fancy?"

"I want my own name," he said dully.

"But it is not permitted."

"Then call me Pigboy. That's the name the bandits gave me."

"Pigboy? How can I insult my younger brother? I am not a bandit."

She had just stolen his precious name, but he did not remind her of that. He simply sat there on the stool staring at the packed earth of the floor.

"All right," she said at last. "If you wish it. But Pigboy is much harder to write than Kuang."

He shrugged. He had no desire to learn such an insulting name. She was stupid if she couldn't realize that. And it would be degrading to learn anything from a woman, not even an old woman, a girl, really. She wasn't even as old as his sisters, hardly older than himself. Well, he would run away as soon as it was safe to do so. She had not, after all, taken back the silver.

"And now," she said, smiling as warmly as she had the night before, "today you must rest. Just before the gates of the city close, we must leave for Thistle Mountain."

So it was that at dusk, while the hundred strokes were being sounded on the gong, they passed through the gates, which closed almost immediately behind them. There were three of them, dressed like peasants in coarse blue cotton, the young woman Mei Lin wearing her great woven straw hat with the false pigtail. Wang Lee had been given new straw sandals to replace the pair he had worn to shreds on the rocky towpaths; otherwise, he wore the same patched clothes his mother had made for him. Their companion was an older man called Chu, stooped slightly by the burdens he had borne across the years. He had ten yellow teeth, none of which met when he smiled, and a twisted face. Each carried a small backpack containing a bowl and chopsticks.

"I was bearing charcoal from the mountains when I was this high," Chu told Wang Lee, indicating with his hand the stature of a small child. "There's a hollow in my back where the basket grew. I was kidnapped by soldiers when I was, oh, I don't know, about eleven. After I escaped, I was an opium carrier for a while. Then back to charcoal. It was in the mountains with a load of charcoal on my back that I first heard the good news of the Heavenly Kingdom. It was our beloved Feng who came to tell us. Feng was the first to believe the Heavenly King's vision. And he came to Thistle Mountain to tell the poor that the High God had made us and cared for us." He reached over and touched Wang Lee's shoulder. "And now, little brother, though you call yourself Pig, you too may cease to be nobody and become a God-worshiper, a child of the Heavenly Father, a citizen of the Heavenly Kingdom."

Mei Lin on her ugly big feet could walk as fast and effortlessly as the two of them. It offended Wang Lee that she should be so manlike. He thought of his mother hobbling daintily about the house and farm. His sisters, too, being the daughters of a landowner, had delicate golden lilies and gentle, high-pitched voices. And even though they were five, six, and eight years older than he, as long as they were at home, his sisters had always shown him the respect due to the eldest son. As far as he could tell, Mei Lin had no respect for any man. Even Old Chu deferred to her.

The district through which they were walking was suffering from drought. It was familiar to Mei Lin and Chu, who knew at sunrise just which farmhouse to approach. The farmer and his wife never failed to greet them warmly, to feed them something, and to offer them the family bed. The three of them slept by day and walked by night. The nights were longer now than they had been when he left Hunan. Wang Lee could tell the difference, or thought he could as they went along, their time of rest shortening as they came closer to Thistle Mountain. He could feel the excitement mounting in the others.

"Won't our little brother be amazed by it all?" Chu asked one night.

"It is hard to imagine," Mei Lin agreed. "At first when Feng formed us into the God-worshiping Society, there were so few of us. We knew only to honor God and his Elder Son Jesus. We despised

idols and the way of wicked people, keeping ourselves pure from the six incorrect deeds. Ah, Chu,
we must teach our little brother the songs which our
Heavenly King wrote to help us keep these things in
our hearts." She began to sing, her clear strong voice
soon joined by Chu's scratchy, unmusical one.
Although they did not sing loudly, Wang Lee was
afraid. Suppose they were heard?

The two God-worshipers sang against the sin of
lewdness. "For those who degrade others are themselves devils." The second misdeed they sang against
was disobedience to parents. Wang Lee felt a pang
of homesickness. There were songs against robbery
and witchcraft and gambling. But the song that
brought Wang Lee wide-awake on his feet was the
song against the killing and maiming of people. "To
kill our fellow men is a major crime, for all under
Heaven are brothers." Then perhaps they would not
kill him if he tried to escape. Perhaps it would be
against their crazy religion. "Worship God," they
were singing, "and you will obtain glory and honor!"

Their songs finished, they turned to him as if to
get once more his approval for their beliefs.

"Good," he said. "Very good." Then, slyly, "Do
you know another one about all men being brothers? I liked that one especially."

"Do you know 'God Is Our Universal Father?'"
Mei Lin asked Chu.

"Of course," he answered and began lustily off-
key, as though not caring now who should hear him
singing in the night. Mei Lin sang too, and to Wang

Lee's untutored ear, it was a beautiful song. In a world in which long-nose foreigners killed Chinese because they refused to poison their nation with opium, where Manchu armies killed Chinese peasants for a handful of rice, and where pirates and bandits killed anyone for no reason at all — in such a world it seemed quite wonderful to him that there were those who sang of human brotherhood and peace.

Yet, even as he marveled, something gnawed at his mind like a mouse at the corner of a rice basket. He felt that Mei Lin was sincere, and certainly he did not doubt Chu; but even in their profession of belief and in their great kindness, there was something that kept him on his guard. Perhaps if Mei Lin hadn't been a woman...

The farther south they traveled, the scarcer food became. Irrigation ditches and ponds were dry ruts and hollows in the cracked earth of the fields.

"It is worse than before," Chu said.

"Perhaps it has rained in the mountains," Mei Lin said. "Often it will rain there while the plains are left to the sun."

That day the hut in which they stayed was deserted. There was nothing left to eat, and they sat on the common bed in the dim light of the mud room, not quite ready to stretch out and try to sleep on empty stomachs. Wang Lee realized that Mei Lin was watching him, and his eyes went, as they had repeatedly, to her feet. She was sitting cross-legged like a boy, and the bottom of her large stained left foot was pointed in his direction.

Perhaps she was a Hakka tribeswoman. Perhaps that was why her feet were unbound. Or the daughter of a poor farmer. Or a slave. But her voice was refined, and she could read and write. He could not put the puzzle pieces together. Who was she?

As if hearing the questions he could not ask, she began quietly to tell him her story.

## CHAPTER FIVE
## MEI LIN'S STORY

"MY FEET WERE NOT BOUND. To this disgrace I owe my life. It is painful for a girl of five to have her arch broken and her toes bent under and bound, but how much more painful to be set aside. My face was plain, the master said, so it was unlikely that I could be sold into a good house or even into a first-class brothel. Better, then, that I remain big footed and thus capable of heavy work.

"Of course, I did not know this in the beginning. As one by one the girls my age in the household had their feet bound, I was patient, believing that my time would come. But one day, I was comforting the youngest daughter of the master's first wife. She was weeping because her little golden lilies hurt so much. 'You are lucky, Mei Lin,' she said. 'You will never have to suffer like me.'

"I was stunned. I went to my mother. She was only a slave, but her face was lovely and her feet had been tightly bound, so she lived as a concubine in this fine house. She had borne the master three sons and was quite a favorite among his women. I threw my arms around her legs and kissed the embroidered shoes upon her beautiful little golden lilies, and begged her to have my feet bound before it was too late. I was already past six, and my feet were growing fast. She did not quite push me from her, but she shook me loose and hobbled away so she would not have to endure my tears. I knew, then, that it was my father, the master, who had decided my fate. As a woman, I was worthless to him. As a beast of burden, I had use.

"At first the insult was so sharp that I stopped speaking. I was afraid that if I opened my mouth, sobs would pour out instead of words. By the time the pain had dulled, I was accustomed to quiet. No one at the house bothered me. They decided I was slow-witted as well as plain. They did not seem to remember that as a little girl I had been the brightest of all the children in the household, that the master himself had said it was a pity I had not been born a boy. Even my mother forgot.

"I was nine years old when the Manchu emperor gave the long-nose foreigners the privilege of free commerce and ceased to oppose the importation of the opium poison into our land. The master, who had been a wealthy merchant, could no longer make a profit. In his worry, he began to take comfort in opium; and then, before long, he ceased to care.

"One by one the pretty girls were sold off, the

boys' tutor was dismissed, the family treasures pawned, the furniture itself began to disappear. One day the mistress, my father's first wife, called me to her rooms. I went in fear, thinking the time had come that I should be sold. And what fate could I hope for, with big feet and a plain face? But it was those very hated feet that saved me. At least for the time being. I was to be sent with the six young sons of the family, including my mother's three boys, to the ancestral farm outside the city. By this time I was twelve years old and a good hard worker. The mistress thought that if she sent me along, her husband's relatives might treat the sons of the family more courteously, might even allow the boys to continue their schooling. Soon the relatives could marry me off to one of the family servants or sell me to a neighboring farmer. In the south, many of the country women have big feet. The Hakka tribe have never bound their daughters' feet, and the Han Chinese have seen how much more profitable a big-footed woman can be on a farm. And although when they become wealthy, the southern farmers may buy themselves a concubine with pale skin and golden lilies, the mistress will be dark-skinned from the sun, and her feet will be nearly as large as her husband's."

Mei Lin could see the contempt in the boy's eyes at the mention of the Hakka. What an arrogant little peasant he was! He had deceived her. When she first saw him in the inn courtyard, she had thought him ready to be one of them. But she was wrong. He was sneering. His nostrils flared out like a horse's.

She would have to warn him about showing his scorn so openly. Or perhaps Chu would explain to him that most of the original members of the God-worshiping Society were Hakka. Indeed, the Heavenly King himself was of Hakka ancestry. And those who were not Hakka farmers were at best unemployed charcoal carriers and miners and at worst former bandits or pirates. It would be hard for such a little mud buddha to understand that it was the Heavenly Kingdom that had conferred nobility upon them — that had given them hope.

"Go on, go on," Chu was urging. He had heard her story before, but he never tired of hearing how those without hope had come into the Heavenly Kingdom.

"It is a long story," she said. "The boy must be tired." Something made her want to stop, to with-hold this part of herself from him. Pigboy indeed. Just by demanding that they call him by a curse word, he had sought to degrade them. "Our younger brother is falling asleep, I'm sure."

"No," said the boy, "I'm not asleep."

"Go on," said Chu again. "Tell about the day you came into the Heavenly Kingdom."

"That was nearly three years after I went to the country," she said. "At first the relatives welcomed me. Not with words, of course, for I was only a slave. But I was put to work, given enough to eat, and treated fairly. The boys, my brothers among them, were allowed to join the sons of the ancestral house in their lessons. All was going well. But then the rains ceased to come. It was as though Heaven had shut its gates against us.

"Now a prosperous household is prepared for one poor harvest, and it can even endure two, if certain economies are taken. I knew that the Patriarch wanted to sell me after the first year of drought. The Matriarch, however, was fond of me. I was quiet and massaged her aching old body and painful little feet. I brought her delicacies from the kitchen, although the cook sought to save them for the Patriarch and his sons. The old woman persuaded the Patriarch to dismiss the boys' tutor instead of selling me. The younger boys were delighted, but my oldest brother was enraged. Despite the fact that he was the second son in the household and not the first, he had a burning desire to become a first degree scholar and an official. He was furious when he learned by household gossip that a female slave — he never thought of me as his sister, the child of his own parents — that a mere female slave was standing in the way of his ambitions. He did not dare to oppose the Patriarch directly, but he wrote to our father's first wife and told her that her son and her stepsons were being deprived of the education she had sent them to the ancestral home to acquire. And all because the Matriarch had taken a fancy to me. Our mistress, as my brother knew, cherished great hopes for her son, so she sent her own personal slave as a gift to the Matriarch, pointing out that the young woman was lovely to look at as well as a skilled masseuse. Of course, her mother-in-law's comfort was of the highest importance, but how much more content she would be seeing that her grandsons become scholars and officials with great power and wealth. They would keep her in luxury as long as she lived on this earth, and sweep her grave and give offerings to her spirit for ten thousand years to come.

"The Matriarch told me sadly that she must let me go. If it were only her present comfort that was to be considered, she would keep me with her. Plain face, big feet, and all, she still preferred me to the little doll my mistress had sent. But it was — couldn't I see? — a much larger issue. It was the future of the family that must be thought of. And besides, the Patriarch would find a good place for me. She was sure of that.

"In the meantime, the drought had continued, and the delay which her first reluctance had caused meant that there were fewer men with money to spend on a new wife or extra slave.

"But there were always soldiers." She stopped. What right did this raw boy have to know? How could he begin to understand her suffering — her deep shame that even yet, after all that had happened, had the power to darken her spirit and drag it down? It was like a deserted well into which some poor soul in anguish had leapt to his death. The well is abandoned, but the body remains, putrefying the water. She shivered. There were still ghosts that even the Heavenly Kingdom had not put to rest.

"I was sold to a local landowner who was also captain of the militia in the district" — she took a breath — "for the use of his men," she finished simply. She did not look at the boy as she spoke, but she could feel him draw back in revulsion. So be it.

"Get on," said Chu. "Now the good part."

"Yes," she said, still not looking up. "Yes. At that same time, Feng was at Thistle Mountain, preaching of the Heavenly Kingdom and forming the God-worshiping Society. The God-worshipers, as you know now, believe in the One True God; so the many idols they saw offended them. They were also grieved at the power these bits of mud and wood and metal had over the common people. They began to smash the idols to show their neighbors the foolishness of these superstitions. They destroyed the most feared of all the images, those in the Temple of Kan-wang, and no gods took vengeance on them.

"But the captain of the militia was angered by this act. And he took his men to Thistle Mountain and arrested Feng and brought him down to the town and put him in a bamboo cage. During the day, the cage was put on display in the marketplace as a warning to people. This would be the fate of any who violated temples or shrines. At night the cage was in the courtyard of his house, near the place where the soldiers were quartered.

"I had heard this story from the soldiers. And one night when they were all dead drunk, I crept out to the cage where Feng was kept, to see this strange fellow the soldiers both despised and feared. The bamboo enclosure was too small to allow a man either to sit up straight or to lie down. He sat huddled over, quietly reciting something to himself as though he were a schoolboy learning his lessons by heart. I stole as close as I could, to hear what he was saying. He was not reciting anything I had ever heard my brothers practice from the five Classics. It was new to my ears. Later he taught it to me." She hugged her knees to her chest and tilted her head back to recite it.

*Out of the depths have I cried unto thee, O Lord.*
*Lord, hear my voice: let thine ears be attentive*
*    to the voice of my supplications.*
*If thou, Lord, shouldst mark iniquities, O Lord,*
*who shall stand?*
*But there is forgiveness with thee,*
*    that thou mayest be feared.*
*I wait for the Lord, my soul doth wait,*
*    and in his word do I hope.*
*My soul waiteth for the Lord more than they*
*    that watch for the morning:*
*I say, more than they that watch for the*
*morning....*

"I realized that he must be reciting some strange prayer of his idol-smashing religion, so I waited for him to finish. But then it became clear that he was repeating the prayer over and over. My heart was touched as I had thought it would never be again, and it gave me courage to approach the cage and ask the man if there were anything I could do for him.

"He turned to me like a man waking from a deep

sleep. It was a few moments before he could focus his eyes on me and reply. 'I thought you were an angel sent from Heaven' he said. And then he asked for a little boiled water, for part of his punishment was to sit in the sun with nothing to drink, and he was very thirsty. I fetched the water for him and waited to serve him further. He tried to send me away. 'If they catch you here,' he said, 'they will punish you.' But I did not believe that there was any punishment worse than what I had already endured without any crime. At last, when he saw I was determined, he asked me if I would risk taking a message to his brothers. He meant his brothers in the society, but I did not know that at the time. The gatekeeper was a kind man, but if my leaving were found out, he might be beaten. So instead of waking him, I climbed the wall like a thief and took Feng's message to his brothers in the next village. They were elated when I told them that the guards were drunk, and came back with me immediately. We climbed in and, with a rope, hoisted Feng, cage and all, over the wall. I realized with joy that they meant for me to flee as well, that in helping their brother I had become one of them. We sawed apart Feng's cage, put him on a wheelbarrow because he was too weak to walk, and went to the mountain that very night."

"And that is how she was saved," said Chu.

"Yes," she said, "that was the night my life began. I have been alive now these three years."

"Good," said the boy, and then, "very good."

She almost despaired. He was stupid as well as

vain. Couldn't he hear how he sounded with his "good, good" every time there was a pause?

Even kind Chu was beginning to sense how little the boy understood. "It is strange," he was saying, "to those who have not heard the Truth, that to the Universal Father women are equal to men. That Heaven" — the old man cocked his head and spoke slowly, with an uncharacteristic formality, to emphasize the importance of his words — "that Heaven does not condemn women who have been used, but rather it condemns the lewdness and cruelty of men who would treat His children so."

"I see," said the boy politely, though neither of them believed he saw anything.

"Mei Lin is a captain in the Heavenly Army," Chu went on. "When the Heavenly Kingdom is established on earth, she will receive property in accordance with her high position and great valor." He waited to let this fact sink in. "In the meantime, we lesser persons must respect and obey her."

"I see," said the boy again. "Yes. I understand."

Chu squinted his already small eyes and tightened his lips as though preparing to carry the matter further. But suddenly he relaxed his gaze and lay down on his side. "We must rest," he said. "If we start early, we can reach the mountain before another dawn."

## CHAPTER SIX
# Lately the Winds Have Greatly Changed

He must have slept or he wouldn't have been jarred by Chu's raspy voice calling him to hurry up. He turned over toward the sound. Both Chu and Mei Lin were standing on the dirt floor, their packs already on their backs. He swung himself over to the side of the bed platform and threw his legs over. His throat was so dry that he did not even try to speak. He felt for his sandals in the near dark and shoved them on, jumping to his feet as he wound his sash around his waist.

"Here." Mei Lin was handing something to him. "Just wet your mouth and throat. It must last all night." He pulled the rag stopper from the container and lifted it to his cracked lips. The boiled water in it was warm and strong with the taste and odor of dried gourd, but the trickle of wetness eased for a moment the painful clawing in his throat. He did not dare take too deep a draft with the two of them staring and waiting. He did take a second quick sip to hold in his mouth and then replaced the rag and returned the gourd to Mei Lin. She tied it once more to her sash.

"Now, my brothers," she said, "sink your teeth into hope and chew on expectation."

Chu laughed. "Two days of hunger will soon be forgotten in ten thousand years of Great Peace." He smacked his lips, proud of concocting a timely proverb. "Good, huh?" he asked Wang Lee.

Unhappily, the boy swallowed the precious water he had been holding in his mouth. "Very good," he muttered, making the old man laugh again.

It was the first night since they had left Kweilin that he had had any difficulty keeping up with his companions. But the God-worshipers were not wasting breath preaching or singing this night. Their noses were bent toward the mountains as oxen's toward the feed trough. Even when they began their ascent, they did not slacken their pace. They made their way in the moonlight along a narrow grass cutters' path, up, up the steep slope. Wang Lee found that his sturdy legs, so used to running and carrying and even towing, were not so accustomed to climbing. The backs of his calves ached, and he longed to stop for rest almost as much as he wanted food and drink. Suddenly, just when he had decided to sit down and let them do with him what they wanted, Mei Lin turned abruptly off the path and went over a crest into a small rocky dip in the hillside.

She knelt down and pushed over a large moss-covered rock. "Heaven is merciful," she said. "The spring still flows."

Wang Lee forgot his tiredness and ran to where she knelt. Without waiting for any permission, he flung himself on the grass and put his whole face into the small pool. He lifted his nose up just high enough to allow his mouth to gulp the cool sweet water in noisy swallows. Long before he had drunk his fill, his head was jerked backward by the pigtail. "Come, come," Chu was grumbling, "others are thirsty, too."

He stumbled to his feet, head down. Mei Lin was laughing at him as she dipped the gourd in the spring and handed it to Chu. "Here, my brother," she said.

"No, sister," the old man said. "After you."

She pressed it on him—Wang Lee could not help thinking that all the exaggerated politeness was for his benefit and then she squatted by the little pool and dipped and drank the water from her cupped hands.

It was another one of her Great Peace preachings, he was sure of that even before she spoke. She seemed determined to humiliate him. "In the Holy Book," she said, "a hero was told by the Heavenly Father to choose an army. He took all the men to a brook and bade them drink. Those who lapped the water with their tongues like dogs, he sent home. The hero could not risk having soldiers so careless of the enemy." Wang Lee's brown face flushed to an even darker shade. But she was not through. "We who belong to the Heavenly Kingdom must be ever on our guard."

He waited for her to rub her lesson in, anger and shame thrashing about in his empty belly, but she had forgotten him. She was patting the rock that she had moved to reveal the spring. Suddenly, she was tearing the moss from it with her nails, and feeling the stone surface with her fingertips. "A message," she explained, and then a shout: "Chin t'ien!"

"Ah," replied Chu, "'Lately the winds have greatly changed.'"

As if she had been given an order by the rock, she rose to her feet, and turning to the southeast, she began goatlike to clamber down the mountain, singing as she went:

> *Lately the winds have greatly changed.*
> *China was conquered but shall be no more.*
> *Heaven intends to raise heroes again.*
> *Brothers, forever must God be adored!*

Chu stooped quickly to refill the gourd, and then he was after her, throwing his rusty voice against her shining one. They seemed not to care in the least whether Wang Lee followed or not. But he did. Where else was he to go?

Long before they reached Chin t'ien, the odor of it reached Wang Lee's nostrils. It was the smell of fires burning in the open, of soup and rice bubbling in iron cooking pots, wonderful smells of cabbage and garlic. The encampment began even on the sides of the mountain, with small tents pitched on what had been rice terraces, and extended down into the plain. They could look in the new light of morning and see below hundreds of figures scurrying about the campfires. No sooner had they approached the first fire than they were greeted warmly, told to present their bowls, and had them filled with soup too hot for even such hungry ones as they to drink.

"There were no lookouts above the camp," Mei Lin said to their host after the meal was finished. "We must not be careless."

The young man smiled. "I thought my sister Mei Lin, of all our people, would spot them."

She looked startled. "Where were they, then?"

"In the grass, behind rocks, in the trees — we've been discovering ways of hiding ourselves in these mountains. Should they threaten us on the plain, we shall need to conceal ourselves like pheasants or field mice up here."

"And all this city spread out below" — she waved her hand to indicate the vast encampment — "what do the district militia make of all this?"

"They are afraid of us, for now. They tell the people we are a religious society — that the Manchu emperor forbids the militia from attacking a religious group. The Imperial army is coming, though. We are seeking some guarantees of freedom. The Heavenly King and Feng have gone to talk with the officials in P'ing-nan."

Mei Lin's eyes clouded. The boy could tell that she was troubled. "And Yang?" she asked. Wang Lee tried to remember who Yang was.

"Ah, Yang. Unfortunately, Yang has fallen ill."

"But Chu and I may report to him? We have messages from the brothers in Kweilin."

The man cocked his head doubtfully. "I do not know," he said. "Perhaps. They say he can neither hear nor speak. But rest your heart, my sister. Feng will return soon, and then…"

They made their way down into the city of tents, Mei Lin asking directions as they went. They learned that Yang was living not in a tent but in the farmhouse of a convert named Wei. Compared to Wang Lee's home, the house of Wei was a mansion, rambling four or five rooms long. Behind it was a pond, shrunken from its banks, but on which ducks still swam. The sound of chickens could be heard in the courtyard. Drought and hunger had not yet captured this place.

Before the courtyard wall of the farmhouse was a bamboo pole from which hung a huge triangular banner with a dragon and phoenix embroidered upon it.

"What does it mean?" Chu asked in a whisper.

"That Yang is second only to the Heavenly King," the girl replied.

"Above Feng?"

She glanced about, as if to see what ears might be close by, then nodded slightly. "So it would appear," she murmured.

At that point a sentry stepped into their path. But before he challenged them, he appeared to recognize them and smiled. "Welcome, my sister and brother. The sun of Heaven shines upon the day of your return."

Wang Lee hung back as his two companions returned the warm greeting. Then they waved him forward and introduced him to the guard.

"A new adherent," Mei Lin said. "We have brought him with us from Kweilin. And now we wish to report to the Tung Wang what we have seen and heard in our half year of wandering toward the north."

"If only that were possible," said the guard. "Yang, our exalted Tung Wang, proclaimed by Heaven to be second only to the Heavenly King himself, fell gravely ill nearly five months ago. He is like one dead, unable to speak or see or hear. Sometimes a watery discharge will flow from his ears, sometimes blood will come forth from his eyes. We pray for his healing morning and evening, but it is Heaven that strikes down and Heaven that raises up."

"Yes," said Mei Lin. "Everything is in the hands of Heaven." Perhaps Wang Lee imagined it, but her tone seemed more brusque than pious.

"I am sure," said the guard, "that the honored Hsiao would welcome your report."

"Hsiao?"

"Our exalted Western King. Since you have been gone this half year, you may not have heard that

Heaven, which chose Yang to be second only to the Heavenly King, did at the same time choose Hsiao to be third."

"And Feng?" Mei Lin's voice was trembling.

"Ah, Feng. The Southern King is a good man, as we all know, but Heaven chooses differently from men. The High God has spoken directly through Yang, and the Elder Brother Jesus has spoken directly through Hsiao. Heaven has not seen fit to give the Divine vision to our brother Feng. He speaks only with his own voice."

"I see," said Mei Lin, but Chu said nothing. They waited in silence while the guard fetched another soldier from inside the house, and then they followed this second one to a smaller farmhouse where the honored Hsiao had his headquarters. The banner before it, though not quite as large as the one before the house of Wei, also bore the royal dragon and phoenix symbols.

Wang Lee was left outside while Mei Lin and Chu went in to give their report to Hsiao. The boy squatted on his haunches on dried earth that had once been a rice paddy. Nearer the river and the irrigation ponds, the fields were still green, but on the dry fields and paddies, tents and lean-tos covered the brown earth. How tired he was! He closed his eyes. Still he could not shut out the camp. The air rang with the sound of smiths pounding metal to metal, carpenters sawing and hammering, women shouting to one another in the fields, children somewhere close by reciting lessons in singsong, and now and again the sound of music, the God-worshipers singing as they worked.

When noon approached, the smell of the campfires and cooking arose, and he was hungry again. But before he could wonder how they would eat, a woman came to him, her head covered by a large straw hat with black cloth hanging from the brim. The hat would have identified her as a Hakka if the large feet had not. She came to him without shyness or hesitation. "Have you eaten yet, little brother?" she asked. He was too hungry now to be polite. When he shook his head, she beckoned him to come to her fire. He took out his bowl and she filled it from her two iron pots with brown rice topped with vegetables. She gave the vegetables a pat with her wooden paddle and then handed the bowl back to him.

He wondered if one thanked women in this strange society, and finally decided it would do no harm. "Thank you, Auntie, I am not worthy of your kindness."

She wiped the sweat off her forehead with the back of her hand and said solemnly, "You must thank the High God. It is He who commands those who have, to share with those who do not."

Once more he was rebuked by a mere woman. But he was not so shamed that he could not eat heartily and belch loudly. His bowl and chopsticks were clean, but he wiped them with his kerchief anyway, because it made him feel prosperous to do so. And after he had replaced them in his pack, he clapped his hands together to thank any stray gods who might be listening.

At long last, Mei Lin and Chu emerged from the small house. Their eyes as well as their lips were quiet, but Wang Lee had been with them long enough to sense their anxiety. He stood up. They did not greet him, but when they got to where he was, Mei Lin flicked her head in command, and he followed them as they walked quickly to the northern extreme of the encampment. It was not until they were out of hearing of the last campfire that they squatted to talk. Mei Lin took off her straw hat, shook out her hair, and then, unexpectedly, buried her face in her hands.

"It may not be as bad as you think," said Chu, sounding like a parent trying to comfort a hurt child.

Wang Lee longed to ask what the trouble was, but he dared not.

"If I could believe that he really cares," she said.

"Hush," said Chu. "Do not take even one sip of disloyalty. It will poison the whole body."

"But if the Heavenly King and Feng are not under arrest, why haven't they returned?"

"It is not for us to know such things...."

"It *is* for us. Heaven means for me to use my head as well as my body."

At the word *body* the old charcoal carrier seemed to become aware of his. "Here," he said. "Give me your bowls, and I will get us some food. We can think better if our bellies aren't growling like tigers."

When Mei Lin made no move, Chu unfastened

the large kerchief which bound up her pack and took out her bowl. Wang Lee started to get out his own — who would know that he'd already eaten? — but something in the girl's misery made him hesitate.

"I was given rice while you were in the house," he said.

Mei Lin looked up. "It's all right," she said gently. "You need more. Let Chu fetch you some. We will need strength." She was not preaching to him so much as appealing to him. She wanted his help whatever the struggle was to be. He bowed his head to her as he handed his bowl to Chu.

"Elder sister," he said, liking her better than he had since he had first known her to be a woman, "my strength, such as it is, is yours."

"The High God's," she said, softening the correction with her smile.

Chu returned, rice bowls stacked into a pagoda. And when they had prayed and eaten in silence and put away their bowls, Mei Lin and Chu began to tell him of their concern.

The Heavenly King and Feng had left the encampment more than a week ago. They were to be with a secret brother in P'ing-nan, a half day's journey to the east. According to spies, a great movement of Imperial soldiers from surrounding provinces was heading in their direction. Could the Manchu have discovered where the Heavenly King was lodged? Were he and Feng already in the hands of the Imperialists? Had the fearful militia taken some action? What was Hsiao about? Why wasn't he making sure of the Heavenly King's safety? What could be the matter with Yang — blind and deaf and dumb, with a disorder no doctor would diagnose? And Feng, dearly beloved Feng, what would become of him, caught between the hatred of his enemies and the apparent ambitions of his brothers?

"We must go to P'ing-nan." Mei Lin's face shone with the decision. "We must know the truth about the Heavenly King and Feng. If they are well, then we will do whatever they command. If they are captured or in danger, then the High God will give us power to deliver them." She was jamming her hair back into her hat as she spoke, ready to leave at once.

"Wait, little sister." Chu stood and put his rough old hand on her arm. "Think. Three will surely be seen more easily than one. I know every pass on these mountains. I know ways to P'ing-nan that no demon soldier ever imagined. Let me go alone. I can go and return by tomorrow."

She nodded and sighed, handing him the water gourd, which he tied to his sash. "I wish I dared ask for food for your journey," she said.

The old carrier belched, making a great show of it and patting his belly afterward. "I have eaten enough for a two-day journey, and here I have only one to go. Rest your heart, little sister." And he was gone before they could wish him well.

## CHAPTER SEVEN
## CHIN-T'IEN

AFTER CHU LEFT, Wang Lee and Mei Lin lay down on the earth to sleep. The autumn sun was warm on the boy's face, his belly was stretched with good warm rice, even his heart was warm. He was too content to feel anxiety for Chu, or for the condition of Mei Lin's beloved leaders, or for his own future. Perhaps, after all, he was only a pigboy, fat and happy as long as there were food and sunshine. How good it was not to be traveling — just to be lying in the sun instead of in a stuffy, flea-ridden hut. And Mei Lin. This morning she had shared her fears with him, had come to despise him a little less. Though why he should care about the opinion of a mere woman, he did not know. But he did care. He sneaked a glimpse at her. She was lying on her back with one arm flung across her face as though to shut out the sun, as though to protect herself. Perhaps, just perhaps, she was not really a thing of iron.

When she woke him, he felt chilled. The sun was sinking fast, and the ground was cold beneath him. He got up quickly.

"Before it is dark," she was saying, "let us see what may be seen."

They made their way to a mound that stood near the farther river at the southern end of the encampment. As they began to climb it, Wang Lee spit three times, making Mei Lin turn to look at him. "You don't need to fear evil spirits on this mound," she said. "See" — she pointed to a great banner that even in the fading light showed the brilliant colors of two dragons and two phoenixes facing a golden sun — "this is where the Heavenly King dwells. The High God will protect this place from demons or wild beasts."

She greeted the sentries by name. They, in turn, knew her and were not ashamed to acknowledge a young woman as their superior.

The sun was crimson over the western mountains, and the two rivers below danced in its reflection. The mountains and rivers embraced the encampment of the God-worshipers like the breast and arms of a loving mother. The night fires began to dot the plain like jewels.

"What do you think?" she asked.

"It's beautiful," he said.

"No, no. How many are there of us, do you think?"

How could he tell? He had never seen a crowd larger than that assembled at a country market.

"Twenty thousand, do you think?"

Twenty thousand. Twenty million. How could he judge?

"Hsiao said that at least fifteen thousand had gathered by the end of August. They have not been able to keep count these last two months." She was standing, feet apart, hands on hips, like a general surveying his troops. Once more, he was a little afraid of her.

"This is only the beginning, you know. The whole world will come to us before the end." She sighed deeply. "In the meantime we must be faithful. Trials will come, but we must not lose heart."

He looked at her. Was she seeing Chu scurrying like a monkey through those mountains? Or beyond, did she see her beloved Feng confined again in a bamboo cage? He wanted to reassure her. "Good" was all he could think of to say.

"Very good," she echoed, smiling wryly. She took leave of the sentries, and they made their way down the mound. People at the nearest campfire called a greeting and invited them to eat. At first she refused, using the polite excuse that they had already eaten, but the family insisted. "We left our bowls at the northern edge of the camp," she said.

"We have bowls and chopsticks to spare," the large-footed Hakka farmwife said. And so they ate rice and cabbage and bits of pork and onion. After they had eaten, they began to sing, and the song he had first heard from Mei Lin and Chu now passed from campfire to campfire, until at last, twenty thousand (could it be?) voices were singing:

*From the first, God is our Universal Father.*
*Like water springing from the earth,*
*    this truth is seen.*
*In the broad mind, all nations are one nation,*
*To the free heart, all strangers are like kin.*
*It is not right that creatures harm each other,*
*So men who kill are lower than the beasts.*
*Seek the harmony of Heaven which bore*
*    and raised us.*
*Live quietly, my brothers, in Great Peace.*

Her plain face came alive when she sang, and there in the shadows with the firelight leaping in her eyes, he almost forgot that she was ugly and unwomanly.

When they rose to go, the Hakka woman brought two quilts from her tent and pressed them on Mei Lin and Wang Lee. They tried to refuse, but she said, "It is according to the command of Jesus, our Elder Brother," so they took them with gratitude.

At their own place, they sat upon their new quilts, but neither felt ready to sleep. They had not slept by night for so long, it seemed strange to them. Nor did the encampment seem to settle for the night. The clang of the smithies still rose in the air.

"They make hoes by day and pikes by night," Mei Lin whispered. "We must be prepared for anything."

Chu was not back by midmorning. They tried not to speak of it or even to think of it. But they did not have enough to keep them busy, and they kept looking over their shoulders toward the mountain, then quickly at each other, and then away.

"Come," she said. "I will teach you. It will pass the time." He was in no mood for straining his mind; but there was nothing else to do, and he could not stand the waiting.

"In the Holy Book, the Heavenly Father has given us Ten Heavenly Precepts which we must respect and obey. Today I will teach them to you. You must keep these precepts forever in your heart."

Inwardly, he groaned. Memorizing the God-worshipers' fancy words. How could he?

"One: Worship only the High God. Two: Do not worship any demon spirits. Three — "

"Wait," he pleaded. "I cannot go so fast."

"I will say all ten at once, and then we will go back over them more slowly." She looked at him fondly, almost as his mother might. "You must hold yourself in patience, little brother."

He tightened his mouth and nodded. He liked her better when she wasn't trying to teach him.

"Three: Do not regard lightly the name of Shang Ti — the High God. Four: Remember to keep the seventh day holy. Five: Be dutiful and obedient to your father and mother. Six: Do not kill or maim people. Seven: Do not commit adultery or harbor lewdness. Eight: Do not steal. Nine: Do not lie.

Ten: Do not be jealous, coveting for yourself what the High God has given to your brother."

He heard the "Ten" and knew she had completed her list; but his mind was a jumble of rules, so he did not look up. She rose to her feet and left him, but before he could wonder where she had gone, she was back with a thin piece of precious firewood in her hands. She squatted down immediately beside him and drew a straight line in the dirt with her stick.

"This," she said, "is the number one." She handed the stick to him. "Now you write it."

He took the stick and drew a line exactly matching hers. "Good," she said. "Now this is the number two." And she drew two lines just under the one. He imitated her lines once again. "This is three," she continued. The warmth spread up from his chest and made his ears tingle. She was teaching him. Not just silly songs and beliefs and rules. She was teaching him how to read and write. Oh, no matter how thick his poor head was, he would learn. He would become the first man in his neighborhood to read and write. He would become a scholar, maybe even an official. He would bring honor to his parents and to the ancient name of Wang. He...

"Four is harder," she was saying. "Watch carefully." She drew the shape of a paddy field and cut off the two top corners. He took the stick tight in his fist, braced his tongue against the corner of his mouth, and drew.

"Not quite," she said gently, taking the stick and scratching away his effort. "Watch, now."

He tried again, the sweat springing up among the unruly hairs that were growing on his once neatly shaven head.

"Good," she said. He looked up in relief. "Very good." They both grinned.

The sun was high. He had taken off his tunic, he was so hot. But in one morning he had learned to read and write all the way to the number ten — so easy, ten, simply a cross mark in the dirt. Wang Lee had forgotten food, forgotten misfortune, even forgotten Chu, until suddenly, there he was, standing over them.

"Pardon the interruption," Chu was saying. They both jumped to their feet.

"Oh, my elder brother," Mei Lin said joyfully. "You have returned to us in safety. God be adored. Have you eaten yet?"

"In truth, not a grain of rice," he said smiling.

Mei Lin quickly collected their bowls. She was Wang Lee's teacher and Chu's superior, but she felt no dishonor in serving them both. Wang Lee was ashamed. He reached out and took the bowls from her. "Thank you," she said. "You need only to walk among the cooking fires with them. Anyone who has more than enough will offer it to you."

He walked into the midst of the encampment as she had directed. The smells, as always, were wonderful. Children darted back and forth across his path, laughing and shouting to one another. Women called out to other women as they chopped and stirred.

Before he had gone a hundred steps, a little girl came running directly to him on unbound feet. "Elder brother," she said, speaking as boldly as a boy, "my mother says to tell you we have rice." She took the tail of his tunic in her small brown hand and led him past two campsites to where her mother stood, ladling rice into the family's bowls.

"Have you eaten yet, little brother?" the woman called in greeting.

"My companions and I have just come to Chint'ien." He felt a need to explain why he was begging food like a mendicant. But she brushed his explanation aside.

"We are all children of Heaven," she said, filling the bowls and stacking them carefully. "You will take care now," she said, handing them back. "Don't spill!"

He promised to walk slowly, thanked her — though she, of course, refused to hear thanks — and went back to where Mei Lin and Chu were pacing back and forth in agitation.

Mei Lin stopped her pacing at the sight of him, hurrying over to take the two top bowls. "Sit down, brother," she directed Chu. "You must eat. Then we will decide what must be done."

The three of them sat upon the earth. Wang Lee had already stuffed himself with a mouthful of rice when he realized that Mei Lin was speaking to her god. He always forgot the praying. There was so much of it. How was a person to remember? Morning, evening, before every bowl of food, sometimes for no good reason at all.

"Have mercy, High God, Heavenly Father, upon us your children...." The prayer went on and on. Wang Lee kept his chopsticks poised and the rice in his mouth, not sure whether to chew or swallow whole. He did not pay much attention to her words — the rice was too sweet upon his tongue — but the tone of her voice was sharp and unmusical. Whatever news Chu had brought, it was not good.

At long last she ceased to pray. Wang Lee quickly swallowed his mouthful while their heads were still bowed and then waited until his elders had taken a bite before taking another one himself.

"Then you think" — Mei Lin was taking up the conversation just where they had left off — "you think it is only a matter of days before the demons attack the house?"

"Why should they wait? They know where Hung and Feng are. They have the place surrounded. Won't they want to attack before we send reinforcements from Chin-t'ien?"

She leaned toward him and spoke in a low voice. "Do you think Hsiao and Yang know?"

"The brothers at P'ing-nan said that word had been sent. They're still waiting for orders."

Mei Lin shivered. "Yang is out of his wits, and Hsiao is... Hsiao will not move without Yang's approval. It is up to us." Her voice had dropped to a whisper. "We must move through the camp like the spring wind, stirring up the people."

Chu unbraided his pigtail and wound a turban around what had been the shaven part of his head.

There was more than an inch of black bristle where it had once been bald. But he only shaved his head and pigtailed the hair growing from his crown when he was spying. Now, as he explained to Wang Lee, they must let their hair grow long all over their heads. Nothing about them must bear the mark of the demon Manchu regime. He unbraided Wang Lee's queue as well and wound a turban about his head. "Your brothers are ready," he said to Mei Lin.

They began at once. Mei Lin went to the tents of the families to gossip with the women. Chu and Wang Lee went to the workplaces of the men and stopped to help a bit at each place, hauling or hammering. If offered, they shared a few sips of boiled water when the men stopped to rest. But always they waited until someone else brought up the matter of Hung and Feng.

"I heard," said Chu slyly, "although you know how rumors are in Chin-t'ien, I heard that the demons have found out the place where the kings are staying and are threatening to attack it. But," he shrugged, "you know how rumors..."

"Then we must go," someone said. "We are many here, and the weapons we make in the night clog the ponds."

"Why do we hesitate?" another asked. "We have nothing to fear from the demon Manchus and their Chinese running dogs."

"I'm sure our leader Hsiao, in his wisdom..."

By evening, when the three of them met at the campfire of their Hakka hosts of the night before, they were greeted with the news. They feigned great surprise, asking what they must do, pledging support for whatever was decided.

On the following day, which was the day before the Holy Seventh Day, the encampment went to work as never before. No command had come down from the farmhouses, but everyone acted as though it had. The camp was preparing for battle. At one point, someone spied a yellow-curtained sedan chair leaving the small farmhouse and being carried to the house of Wei. Chu elbowed Wang Lee who was beside him, harvesting cabbages. "It is Hsiao," Chu said, hardly moving his lips. "He is going up to see Yang."

The next morning, the families in the camp gathered into their units of twenty-five families for Sabbath worship. Since the three companions belonged to no family organization, Mei Lin decided that they would go to the service on the mound.

The tents had been cleared to make a broad place for the service. There were log benches in two separate rows with an aisle between. The men sat down on one side and the women and children on the other. Somehow Wang Lee was surprised to see Mei Lin go to the women's side. There were other women dressed as manlike as she. Most all the women had large feet, but there were, he could see out of the corner of his eye, a few bound feet even among the God-worshipers.

The hymn was beginning. He stood with the

others, though he seemed to be the only one who did not know the song.

*Lift up your heads to the heavens:*
*See sun and moon and stars and cloud.*
*See thunder, rain, and wind*
*All these are miracles from God.*
*Look down upon the earth:*
*See mountain, river, marsh, and plain,*
*The birds of air, the fish of sea,*
*All creatures from His hand....*

The eyes of all assembled were on the worship leader at the front. But Wang Lee was aware of something happening on the path. He dared turn his head a fraction to the left. Something large and yellow was coming up. It was a sedan chair, curtained about with yellow silk and decorated with a single dragon and phoenix. So it was one of the two kings, either Hsiao or Yang, coming to the service on the mound.

The singing continued, but more than one pair of eyes turned to stare at the chair, and Wang Lee could feel a ripple of excitement pass through the God-worshipers. The chair was carried to the very front and center of the congregation. The volume of the hymn rose to its climax:

*God be forever and ever adored!*

As the word *adored* rang in the air, the silken curtains opened. There was a gasp from the whole assembly. The man who stepped out from between the curtains was shorter than Wang Lee. His long hair hung all about his shoulders and was topped with a yellow turban. A sparse mustache bristled across his upper lip. His eyes were deeply sunk in a face roughly pocked with smallpox scars. He wore a long yellow robe, embroidered with the dragon and phoenix.

"God be adored!" the worship leader cried out. "Our beloved Yang, our great Tung Wang, is among us!"

A cheer went up from the congregation. There were shouts of "Yang! Yang!" "Glory to the High God!" "God be adored!"

"It is a miracle!" cried the worship leader.

"A miracle of God!" responded the worshipers.

Yang stood silently before them. As short and as ugly as he was, there was a spirit about him. Wang Lee held on to his own small soul. He had been with Mei Lin and Chu too long not to fear this little man standing there, accepting the shouts of the people.

The Eastern King looked heavenward and held his hands stretched up to the sky. The crowd on the mound grew suddenly quiet, so quiet that the hymns and prayers from the other services could be heard as a murmur across the plain below. Yang kept his heaven-directed pose as the tension about him grew. Wang Lee felt a hand grasping his arm. It was the man on his left, staring at the figure of Yang, but holding on to Wang Lee as though the man might be sucked up into the sky if he let go. Wang Lee's own heart began to pound. Just when he thought it might burst from his tunic into the silence, Yang flung his hands out and looked the congregation in the face. His neck muscles began to twitch. The throng waited, hardly breathing. A strange scratching sound began in his throat. It was an animal sound, like that of a dog retching, but no one moved, no one spoke.

"G-g-g-g-ah, G-ah-ah, G-o-d be adored." It came out at last, only a hoarse whisper. Still the silence held.

Then, suddenly, the worship leader threw his arms in the air. "God be adored!" he cried. "God be adored! The Tung Wang speaks!" He shrieked out the first line of a hymn, which the congregation joined. They were singing louder and faster with every line, the small dark eyes of Yang fixed upon them, stirring them more and more. At the end of one hymn, another was begun. A woman leapt into the center aisle and started to dance. The man who grasped Wang Lee's arm held on so tightly now that the pain was hard to bear, and yet it kept the boy's heart from flying to pieces inside his chest.

Suddenly the Tung Wang thrust his right hand toward them, palm spread. At once the singing stopped. The woman sank back to her place. The man's hand dropped from Wang Lee's arm.

"God be adored," the little king said, his voice scratchy but soft.

"God be adored," the congregation responded

quietly. "My brothers and sisters," Yang said, "Heaven has healed me."

"A miracle of Heaven!" a voice cried out.

"Yes." Yang's voice was still soft. "A miracle from the High God. I have been tested and found true and worthy." He paused to look back and forth across the congregation. "There is a great task before us, my brothers and sisters. Are you also true and worthy?"

Cries of "Yes!" "True and worthy!" came back in reply.

Yang nodded his acceptance of the cries and then motioned again for silence. "God has come down to earth," he said. "The word of Heaven has come to me. I saw in a vision our Heavenly King, surrounded by demons." He waited and let the murmur of distress run through the assembly, "I go!" His voice rose like the roar of fire. "I go as Heaven's messenger to save him. Who will go with me?"

"I go!" "I! I!" "Let me go!"

"Spread the word throughout the camp," he said, his voice now strong and powerful as thunder. "At dawn we march. All commanders and captains will meet at the house of Wei at sunset when the Sabbath is past. God be adored!"

"God be adored!" They screamed the reply. Wang Lee heard his own voice lifted with the rest and began to shake.

The Tung Wang climbed between the silken curtains. The four chair bearers hoisted the chair effortlessly to their shoulders. The worship leader began to sing:

*Lately the winds have greatly changed.*

With one voice they took it up:

*China was conquered but shall be no more.*
*Heaven intends to raise heroes again,*
*Brothers, forever must God be adored!*

Still singing, the worship leader took his place at the rear of the sedan chair, and all the God-worshipers fell into place behind him. They marched down the hill past other groups of worshipers, who, realizing that some great event had taken place, joined the march. The sedan chair swung off the path and headed back to the house of Wei, but the worship leader led the marchers, still singing, toward the southern river.

It was a chilly autumn day, and when Wang Lee saw that the crowd was moving straight for the river, he tried to hang back. But he was carried forward by the stream of march, right into the icy waters. The God-worshipers ducked beneath the surface and came up with shouts and prayers. Wang Lee stood waist deep in the water and watched, shivering. He could not swim, and he was terrified someone might push him past his depth. There were so many people thrashing about, not caring what they were doing.

"Hold your breath," a hoarse voice said in his ear. But before he could do so, he was pulled under and out. He sputtered and coughed, the water burning his nose and throat. Chu was holding his arm, dragging him to shore.

"Sorry, little brother," the charcoal bearer was mumbling under the frenzied cries of the crowd. "You can't just stand there. No true believer would."

When they got back to the place they had claimed for themselves, Mei Lin was waiting, sitting cross-legged on the ground, squeezing and rubbing her long hair, smiling so broadly that it was almost rude.

"God be adored!" she called out to them. But when they were close to her, she added quietly, "Good work, my brothers."

## CHAPTER EIGHT
## TO THE AID
## OF THE KINGS

HE WAS AWAKENED by the smell of a steamed pork dumpling positioned directly below his nose. He jerked to a sitting position. Both Mei Lin and Chu were laughing. "I told you," Mei Lin was saying. "One sniff of pork dumpling, and we would have his full attention."

"Where did you get meat?"

"See," she said. "Not, 'What are our orders?' or 'When do we march?' but 'Where did you get meat?'"

She was deliberately shaming him, laughing at his greediness. Chu was laughing too, but differently, his eyes wrinkled with kindness in his twisted face. Wang Lee got to his feet and slipped on his sandals (the river had not been kind to them). He busied himself wrapping his sash about his waist, and then, still not looking at them, he retied the turban that now covered at least part of his unkempt hair. He wished fleetingly that the God-worshipers weren't so stubborn about queues. The hair growing about his crown was longer than Chu's, but it grew straight up like broomstraw, and the long hair that had once been a neat pigtail now fell to his shoulders in a tangled mass. He was glad his father could not see him. He cleared his throat and spit, not toward either of them, of course, but just to hint that he was tired of their laughter.

Chu grew sober at once, but Mei Lin didn't even notice his gesture. The girl was still laughing as she and Chu squatted on their heels to eat. They had somehow found enough charcoal for a fire and were boiling water in a tiny brass teakettle. Wang Lee hesitated for a moment, caught between pride and hunger and a third feeling — a fear that they might shut him out of their happiness. He started toward the fire. Mei Lin looked up. "Hurry," she said. "We have good food and much to do before morning."

She placed three steamed dumplings into each bowl, said the prayer before meals a little faster than usual, and then they fell to the feast. "Slowly," she said. "Eat slowly. It is a waste to eat good food too fast." But they could not help themselves. When they had finished, the dumplings gone far too quickly, she took from her sash a small bag. "Hold out your bowls," she said. And when they did, she dropped a pinch of tea leaves into each one and then poured on boiling water.

At first they drank in only the aroma of the tea, passing their bowls back and forth before their noses to assure themselves that it was truly tea and giving it time to steep to amber, the smell growing richer with the color. "Where did you get..." Wang Lee stopped mid-question, but she was already laughing.

"'Where did you get meat? Where did you get tea?' Where," she asked mischievously, "did you get cloth shoes with thick soles for marching?"

She was surely teasing now. He said nothing in reply, taking a noisy sip of the scalding tea to protect himself against her.

"It is true," she said. "There are cloth shoes for each of us and — and weapons."

A chill went through him. Weapons meant fighting. He had no taste for soldiering. It is not right that creatures harm each other. Didn't their own song say so? Why were they marching with weapons?

"Yang will not go to P'ing-nan after all. The armies of Yang and Hsiao will hold Chin-t'ien. The women with children, all the young, the weak, the old will stay here under their protection. But we," she said joyfully, "we in the armies of Feng and Wei go to free the kings. Feng is not here to lead us, but his commanders order us to join together exactly as if he were. When we see him again, we must show that his people were united even in his absence. So" — she was wiping her bowl as she stood up — "move quickly. We must pack and join the others at the base of the mound. Our army will lead the assault, in honor of the Heavenly King and our beloved Feng, who is sharing his danger."

The pork dumplings were turning against the floor of the boy's stomach as he wrapped his bowl and chopsticks in his quilt and tied them into a pack. He could not even enjoy the feel of the new cloth shoes on his feet. They meant marching, and at the end of marching...? It was not like killing a chicken or pig, that much he knew. The beasts, after all, do not fight back.

As if reading his thoughts, Mei Lin emerged from the darkness into the flickering light, carrying two bamboo poles with sharp metal points lashed to the ends. She solemnly handed a pole to each of them.

"Because I am a captain," she said almost apologetically, "they have given me a sword."

"Where are the guns?" This burst out without Wang Lee's intending it to. He had seen Imperial soldiers. He knew they had guns. What could bamboo sticks like these do against guns?

She laughed again. "They gave me meat dumplings and shoes. How could I dare ask for more?" She took the crude pike from him and began to tie it to his pack. "There," she said, "try walking. See if it is comfortable for you." She proceeded to tie Chu's pike to his pack. "Besides," she added, "have you ever used a gun? Would you know how?"

When the first streaks of red slashed the darkness over the rivers, the marching song began. The chosen band of God-worshipers, male and female, moved forward. Mei Lin, Chu, and Wang Lee followed almost immediately behind the dragon and tiger banner of Feng, the Southern King, marching through the valley of the Hsuan River toward P'ingnan. Along the way they were joined by farmers carrying hoes and bandits carrying daggers or long swords. Some who joined them were bare-handed. But before they had gone far, the dust of their marching clouding the morning air, they came in sight of the enemy, a body of Imperial troops who had been sent to meet them.

A gong was struck and the order to attack swept through the God-worshipers. Wang Lee felt himself carried forward, as he had when they had all rushed for the river. A calm voice was saying inside his head, "I am going to die. I am going to die in the brown dust of Kwangsi, far from the graves of my ancestors. I am nothing more than a pig for the slaughtering." Without feeling, his legs ran. The screaming of the mob bore him forward like the force of a flood.

Suddenly, before him, the wall of government troops began to crumble. The men in uniform — the men with guns — were turning and running. Shots were being fired, but they seemed unreal and far away. The tail of his turban was streaming straight behind him as he ran, pike in hand. His cotton-shod feet hardly touched the ground. His own throat took up the battle cry. The enemy were running, showing their heels to a ragtag peasant army.

It was like a game played by children. They chased the silly boys to the river, where the cowards leapt to the decks of their boats and fled downriver, out of reach of homemade spears and swords.

A great shout went up, exploding into a hymn of praise. The God-worshipers chanted a prayer of thanksgiving, and then set up camp to eat and rest. A rumor spread from campfire to campfire that on the Sabbath, God had descended from Heaven and given Yang a vision that only now could be revealed. The High God had told Yang that the God-worshipers would be protected from all harm in battle. Their bodies would be surrounded by Heavenly armor that bullets could not pierce or swords cut through. Indeed, when the field of battle was cleared, the few corpses that lay there were in government dress.

Chu was exultant because he had picked up a matchlock gun thrown down by a fleeing demon. The soldier had not, in his haste thrown down powder or plug or ball or match to go with the gun, but Chu would not be teased about it.

"Heaven will provide," he said, spitting on the metal barrel and polishing it with his kerchief. This time it was Wang Lee who laughed with Mei Lin.

They had assumed, as the victorious always do, that they would march on immediately, that they would move at once to P'ing-nan and to the release of the kings. But from somewhere above, caution was demanded. Scouts were sent ahead. Word came back that the Imperialists were strengthening their forces in P'ing-nan, that troops were hurrying in from all the neighboring districts.

The God-worshipers withdrew toward the mountains, where the charcoal bearers and miners among them knew every crevice and undulation of the land. Looting and rape were crimes punishable by death. So when they marched, they stayed upon the paths between fields and paddies, destroying nothing, taking nothing, asking nothing. The farmers, so used to the abuses of government troops, ran after them, bringing gifts of grain and vegetables and even meat. Those who had nothing to give came themselves to join the God-worshipers' holy army.

They sheltered themselves against the late autumn wind in mountain caves. Mei Lin was restless, eager to move on. After all, she had saved Feng before almost single-handedly. It was natural that she be impatient with talk of waiting for more troops, better weapons. But Wang Lee only wished that their mountain sojourn could continue on and on. They had each been given warm padded jackets, and there was food every day. Besides, Mei Lin was teaching him to read and write. She was trying to teach Chu as well, but the old charcoal bearer had not much brain for it. Wang Lee felt quite clever by comparison. It took the boy time to get a character firmly established in his head. But once there, it would stay as though mortared in place. But poor Chu, the characters flowed through his mind like mountain water in springtime. No matter how hard he tried, he could not keep hold of a character for more than a day.

Late in December the long-awaited orders came. They were to march, climb rather, down to P'ing-nan. The Imperialists were expecting them to march through the river valley as before, so the God-worshipers took the treacherous mountain paths instead. They tore their quilts into strips, and bound them about their legs. Bright pieces, red ones especially, were used to make new turbans for their heads. Heaven had not yet sent Chu his ammunition, but he strapped both matchlock and pike to his back. No duck could have been prouder of her duckling than he of that old gun.

This time instead of hymn and war cry and noonday sun, there were steep slopes to creep down at night, and only the moon for light. They had waited in the mountains for more troops from Chin-t'ien, but Wang Lee never understood why; because when they neared the enemy lines, only a few men were sent out at a time. They moved like owls through the darkness, swooping down and killing quickly, without sound. If there were any battles, Wang Lee was not aware of them. Mei Lin chafed, but they were moving forward inch by inch. And Chu, who had come this way many times before, assured them that all was well. But then Chu was one of the owls of night. The commanders were sending out only those who knew the terrain.

They were near P'ing-nan. The rumor spread through the God-worshipers that they were less than three li from the place where the Heavenly King and Feng were being detained. A night of no moon was chosen for the attack. The owls were sent first to pick off the sentries. Then the armies of

God-worshipers crept forward toward the dim lights of the house.

A soldier appeared at the door, rifle at the ready, peering out into the darkness. From the night came a yelp, like that of a fox. When the guard turned toward it, a rebel leapt on his back, bringing him to the earth without a sound. The rebel quickly put on the guard's blousy tunic and trousers, picked up his rifle, and entered the house. The dim light disappeared. A small, uncurtained sedan chair was brought forward for the Heavenly King to ride in, but Feng walked with the troops. Within minutes, the God-worshipers were on their way again, homeward across the mountains.

When Wang Lee first saw the two kings by the light of morning, he was secretly disappointed. Neither was very tall, though Feng seemed the taller of the two. Swinging along in the sedan chair, the Heavenly King looked more like a stocky Hakka farmer than the Younger Son of the Heavenly Father. His brown face was smooth and broad. He wore a yellow turban on his long hair and had a sparse beard growing on his chin. He wore no kingly robe such as Yang had worn. Instead he had on a long blue robe over trousers that one might see on an itinerant scholar in any market village.

Feng was more the shape of a scholar, gracefully slender. His hair and beard were full and black. It was only when the three companions came near to greet him that Wang Lee could see his face. It was young, with warm, gentle eyes. The affection in his voice when he spoke to Mei Lin was unmistakable, almost indiscreet.

"I knew Heaven would send you again, my sister," he said.

From Mei Lin's conversation, Wang Lee had pictured an elderly Feng, a white-bearded venerable. That this handsome young figure was the beloved Feng was, well, not an altogether pleasant surprise. The boy mumbled something when Mei Lin introduced him, and was grateful when the audience was over and he could follow Chu back to their place in the line of march.

"The Southern King has a wife, you know," Chu said.

"Why tell me this?" The kindly Chu could be annoying.

"Ah, no reason."

Later Mei Lin, her face glowing like the fullest moon of autumn, caught up with them. "He is well," she said. "God be adored."

The God-worshipers sang most of the way back to the encampment at Chin-t'ien, where they were greeted with shouts of joy by those who had stayed behind. The shouting had hardly died when the Imperialists attacked. The demons came by way of both rivers, but the God-worshipers were ready for them. The few guns the rebels had were used to pick off soldiers who attempted to scale the banks of the rivers. Those who managed to escape the guns were run through with pikes by a screaming line of God-worshipers.

Wang Lee, stationed on the mound with the rest of Feng's army, looked down on Yang's troops who were leading the charge. Perhaps the rebels were protected by Heaven. They rushed fearlessly at the foe who broke and ran, even when the Manchu commanders fired at them to stem the retreat. The outcome was never in question. The God-worshipers held their ground and forced the government troops back into their boats. The enemy rowed rapidly out of sight to the music of the rebels' hymns of triumph.

Perhaps being a member of the God-worshipers' army was not as bad as Wang Lee had feared. Below him, Yang's troops were clearing the riverbank. They seemed to be picking up a variety of guns as well as swords, long and short. From the distance of the mound, it was like a theatrical being played out below — now lifeless forms were being dragged down the bank to a distance well south of the mound. Later, when the wind was from the north, they would be burned. But the boy did not know that at the time.

Wang Lee was a veteran of three battles without ever once having thrust his pike in the direction of an enemy soldier. It was not until nightfall, when he made his way down from the mound, that the battle became real for him. There in the light of the supper fires he saw them: pikes planted into the riverbank, from which a row of bloody heads grinned down upon the camp. He started to spit against the demon spirits of the place, but found himself retching instead.

Around the fires, families were having their evening prayers and singing, or did he just imagine it?

> *It is not right that creatures harm each other,*
> *So men who kill are lower than the beasts.*
> *Seek the harmony of Heaven which bore*
> *and raised us.*
> *Live quietly, my brothers, in Great Peace.*

Mei Lin and Chu were beside him. She offered him a rag with which to wipe his face. He took it, ashamed that a woman should see his weakness but comforted to have his friends close.

## CHAPTER NINE

# THE NEW AGE

IF THERE HAD BEEN any doubt before, the battle of Chin-t'ien convinced the God-worshipers that the Mandate of Heaven had fallen upon Hung. When a dynasty forgets virtue, when the powerful begin to grow fat upon the flesh of the weak, nature itself rebels. Earthquakes, floods, famine, pestilence, and drought occur, and the wise man knows that the time is ripe for revolution. Heaven has withdrawn its approval from the present regime and is ready to pass on its mandate to one that is worthy.

The kings met in council and decided that the thirty-seventh birthday of Hung, falling on the tenth day of the twelfth moon (or the eleventh of January 1851, according to the long-nose calendar), would become the first Day of the New Age. The new dynasty would be called Taiping Tienkuo — the Heavenly Kingdom of Great Peace. Hung was the Tien Wang — the first Heavenly King. He would not be emperor. The High God alone would bear that title. But Hung, as Son of Heaven and younger brother of Jesus, would serve as the High God's regent on earth.

The time until the celebration was short, a little more than a week, so the encampment fell into a fever of preparation. All monies and valuables that had not already been gathered into the central treasury were called in at this time. Mei Lin had a little silver and two strings of cash left from her trip north. Chu had nothing. Wang Lee still had the silver Mei Lin had given him in Kweilin. He hoped she'd forgotten, but of course she had not. He handed it over with a feeling that his last escape route had been cut off. He was a God-worshiper now, whether he wanted to be or not. So when Mei Lin suggested that he undergo the ritual of baptism in honor of the proclamation of the new dynasty, he could not refuse.

Mei Lin gave up teaching him to read and write in order to pound as many rules and notions as possible into his head before the great day. "If only Feng could instruct you," she kept saying. But the beloved Feng was forever at the house of Wei, which was now the headquarters of the Heavenly King. Feng, the scholar, was composing and writing many of the declarations of the new kingdom. "But Feng has promised to baptize you himself," said Mei Lin, as though he should be grateful that she had obtained this favor.

Wang Lee hardly believed that it would happen.

Why should Feng take time from the great preparations to bother with him? Yet on the Sabbath, he was summoned, along with other baptismal candidates, to the small farmhouse. Feng himself presided. The seating was divided as usual, with the sexes separate, and Mei Lin went over to sit with the women. Chu took Wang Lee to the front bench on the men's side. The room was dark, lacking even the paper-covered windows most small farmhouses possessed. The only daylight came from the doorway at their rear. At the front was a table on which sat two crude lamps — burning wicks floating in peanut oil — and three teacups. Before the table stood Feng, looking taller and more handsome than Wang Lee remembered.

Chu was nudging him with an elbow. He stopped staring at Feng long enough to look at Chu, who was waggling his chin, indicating that Wang Lee was to stand up with the other candidates. He stumbled awkwardly to the front. There were ten of them. Feng was reading their names from a list. Wang Lee listened in vain for his own name. It was not until sometime later that he realized Mei Lin had given the name of Huang to be used as his baptismal name, not willing to have him baptized as Pigboy.

The others were repeating something after Feng. Oh yes. They were saying the sins that they had been required to submit in writing. What had he confessed to? Greed, he recalled. Idolatry. The uttering of falsehoods. Had he listed pride? He remembered Mei Lin had suggested it. Perhaps people always saw their own sins in others. When the group finished their squirrel chatter of confessions, Feng turned and put the paper containing their baptismal names and written confessions over the lamp wick. The paper blazed up. "Thus," said Feng quietly when the paper was brown ash on the table, "do you offer up to Heaven your lives and confessions."

"And now," he said, turning back to the candidates, "do you promise not to worship evil spirits nor to practice evil things, but to obey with your whole hearts the Heavenly Precepts?"

They answered yes and then began to recite the precepts. Wang Lee was good at the numbers, but he could hardly remember which commandment followed which, and he looked at his feet and mumbled in echo throughout the recitation. The others then knelt, but Wang Lee didn't get the signal immediately and was scrambling to his knees a few embarrassing seconds after the others. He closed his eyes. His face was burning. He felt that he might suffocate, it was so stuffy in the small mud room. Feng was coming down the row toward him, followed by someone else. Wang Lee kept his head bowed, trying to hide his burning cheeks. Before he knew what was happening, Feng had reached a cup into the basin carried by his assistant, dipped out a cupful of cold water, and poured it onto Wang Lee's head. It rushed down front and back, soaking him thoroughly. Feng was chanting something about the Father, Son, and Holy Ghost, and purification from all former sins, and becoming a new person.... Why were there so many surprises? Mei Lin had told him about baptism, but she hadn't prepared him for the pouring of cold water all over him in the depths of winter. Feng had completed the row. The newly baptized God-worshipers stood up again. Feng and his basin bearer came back down the row once again, handing each in turn a cloth. This time Wang Lee watched carefully. Each man was opening his tunic and washing his chest with the cloth before returning it with a bow to Feng, who rinsed it in the basin, squeezed it out, and handed it to the next in line. Then the tea was passed down the line, and each man took a sip before giving it to the next.

When this was done, the whole congregation turned around and knelt, facing toward the light from the doorway. And Feng prayed, not only for the newly baptized, but for the whole company of God-worshipers and the new dynasty that would soon be born. They left the service singing and, to Wang Lee's great distress, marched directly to the river. It couldn't be helped. He would freeze to death on this, the first day of what had promised to be his new life. There was no escape. He marched to the river as he had marched to battle, resigned to his death — right into the icy waters. He ducked himself, not waiting for Chu to half drown him; and then, finding he could still move, got out of the water as fast as he could.

Mei Lin was standing on the bank with a quilt in her hands that she wrapped around him. "God be adored!" she said joyfully.

He nodded. His teeth were chattering so that he couldn't speak.

The next few days were like a gigantic preparation for the New Year. And, as Mei Lin said more than once, it was not simply a New Year, but a New Dynasty, a New Age. He would never know how the God-worshipers managed to collect so much food. The area was supposedly suffering from drought and near famine, but food there was. The three companions were given rice, vegetables, oil, salt, tea, even half a chicken and a bit of pork. Wang Lee, who had not cooked since he left the bandits, found himself cooking once more under Mei Lin's careful supervision. Chu kept the fire going and carried water for them. No one expected an old charcoal bearer to know how to prepare feast food, but he tried to keep them laughing with his stories.

He loved to tell of the magic Monkey who stormed the citadels of Heaven and Earth, demanding from the Immortals a giant brush so that he could stroke the date of his death from the Book of Life and thus live forever. Then, when he was given an audience with the Emperor of All China, he looked about the Yellow Palace of the Eternal City and sniffed. "What a pity. I have a nice tiled house, while His Majesty must live in a place the very color of jaundice!"

"No, no," Mei Lin protested even while she laughed. "You shouldn't fill the boy's mind with those silly stories of the past. Tell us a story to improve our characters."

"Let's see." Chu tilted his head as he poked the charcoal to glow. "Improve your characters, eh? Well, how about a story against laziness?"

Mei Lin looked doubtful, but there was no stopping Chu. "We must beware of laziness," he said solemnly. "Remember the farmer who married a lazy, lily-footed woman who would do no work, not even cook rice for herself and her husband? Despite this, the foolish farmer loved her. One day it was necessary for him to go on a long journey. It would be another moon or two before he could return. The farmer was afraid that his lazy wife would perish while he was gone. At last he had a wonderful idea. He made an enormous doughnut and put it on her head. All she would have to do when she was hungry was take a bite. Thus, putting his heart to rest, he set out. But alas, when he returned, he found his wife dead. Despite his precaution, she had starved to death. She had eaten the part of the doughnut directly in front of her face but was too lazy to turn it."

Laziness was not a vice the God-worshipers need fear. Wang Lee did not mind the work, but he longed for the leisure to continue his lessons. By the time he stopped at night, there was no light, even if he had the energy, by which to scratch characters in the dirt and memorize them. But on the eve of the great day, Mei Lin gave him a present. He protested. He had nothing to give her in return, but she pressed the kerchief-wrapped parcel upon him. It was a book. He opened it carefully, and happiness exploded in his chest like a string of firecrackers. He could read it — at least he could read the first few pages. It was the primer the God-worshipers had printed for their children. It contained all the basic characters that Mei Lin had pounded into his head.

"One," he read aloud, his hands and voice shaking. "One: Worship only the High God. Two: Do not worship any demon spirits...."

"Not even with a spit," she said.

He laughed. A man who could read did not need to spit at demons. The characters opened themselves up to him like gates swung open by unseen keepers. Those mysterious strokes upon a page were now words, with meaning and beauty, into which he, Wang Lee, could enter and feast.

Oh, if only his father could see him now, hear him reading from a book. "I will learn everything written here," he said, clutching the book close. "I will treasure every character in my heart."

"Good," she said.

"Very good," echoed Chu.

The first day of the New Age was greeted with the staccato bursts of fireworks, the booming of hundreds of gongs, and hymns of praise rising from thousands of throats. It was noise to shake the mountains and chase the rivers to the sea. At noon the God-worshipers gathered around the mound, arranged in units of a leader and twenty-five families, to receive the declaration from the Heavenly King. Since there were thousands of ears and only one Heavenly Mouth, the printing presses had provided a copy of the King's words for every unit, so that the unit leader could read the declaration at the same moment that Hung was proclaiming it from the mound.

Wang Lee stood with Mei Lin and Chu, trying to keep his hand from fingering his book, which he had tucked into his sash. He didn't like it to be out of his sight. This morning he had learned the characters for *Heavenly Kingdom of Great Peace* in honor of the day. *Great* — a man with arms stretched wide. *Peace* — a woman under a roof. "You see," Mei Lin had said, "that is why we God-worshipers say that a man can have only one woman. We believe in peace." Chu was poking him. He must fix his gaze on the leader and try to listen.

The voice of the leader droned on and on — elaborate explanations of who was to be king of what. The only thing that came clear to Wang Lee was the fact that Yang and Hsiao were now officially elevated above Feng. Feng was number three under the Heavenly King, even though he had been teacher to them all, despite the fact that before he had preached the Good News to them, Yang and Hsiao had been only ignorant charcoal bearers and sometime bandits.

He stole a glance at Mei Lin. Her face was as smooth as a teacup. If she were eating bitterness, no one would know it. Her eyes were steady, as though fully in accord with the declaration.

The leader read on. Soldiers were to obey the Ten

Heavenly Precepts and related rules. They were never to trouble civilians. They were to obey every order. They were never to retreat without specific command. And, until the Heavenly Kingdom triumphed, men and women were to be strictly separated.

Now Wang Lee was listening, as were they all. Women, girls, and small boys under the age of ten would live in the western part of the camp, and men and older boys would live in the eastern. There were to be no mixed battalions in combat. For the sake of the Heavenly Kingdom, which would last ten thousand years, they must remain, for this brief period, separate, celibate, and pure of heart. "You must respect this!" leaders all over the encampment cried, echoing the Heavenly King's command that summed up the declaration.

The three companions did not speak of the orders when the declaration was ended. They joined in the singing and watched the sacrifices. Perfectly good dog meat was being burned as an offering to the God-worshipers' deity. Even though Wang Lee had been baptized by Feng himself, he still could not understand the craziness — jumping into rivers in the middle of winter, burning good food, allowing women to become soldiers, and now, separating families and friends.

The three of them soberly ate their feast food. It would be their last meal together, perhaps for many years. No one wanted to talk about it, but finally Chu burst out, "My sister, you are the only family I can remember."

She put down her bowl and laid her chopsticks across the top and stared at them. "It is only until Nanking," she said.

The old man sighed and made a snuffling sound in his nose.

"Surely I will see my brothers from time to time in passing. I will need to know that you go in good health."

"But who will teach us?" Wang Lee hadn't meant to blurt out the question.

She looked him in the face. "You have your book now, and you can have others when you need them. You can teach yourself, or if you find a new character that you cannot break down into its parts and decipher, you have only to ask. Everyone is willing to teach. We are all brothers and sisters. You know that."

Yes, thought Wang Lee, brothers and sisters. She forgets that it was her own blood brother who had her sold to be a soldiers' whore.

# CHAPTER TEN
## SOLDIER IN THE HEAVENLY ARMY

IT WAS INDEED A NEW LIFE FOR WANG LEE. Before the declaration of the New Age, he had been a boy, a greedy peasant oaf—a pigboy. Now, suddenly, he had become a man, a soldier in the Heavenly Army, destined not only to free China from the Manchu demons but finally, under the Mandate of Heaven, to rule the world.

Even nature proclaimed their just cause. The rain, which for three years had refused to fall, began in earnest. The Gates of Heaven were flung open, the rain poured down. Nothing could have helped the Heavenly Army more. Their ranks were full of men like Chu—charcoal bearers, grass cutters, miners—who knew every inch of Thistle Mountain and its surroundings. When government troops came to harry them at Chin-t'ien, they simply withdrew through the mists to the mountain. There they hid themselves like field mice until some daring enemy unit made a sortie up a pass, and then the rebels pounced, more tiger than mouse. Soon no Imperial troops would come into Taiping territory unless the orders were reinforced by guns pointed at their backs.

In February, Wang Lee killed his first man. It was dark, and raining as usual. The rebels waited behind bushes just above the path where ten soldiers, strung out by the hard climb, were slowly moving. The rebels leapt down on the demons, who did not have time to get the guns off their backs.

Wang Lee could not see the man's face. He felt the hard resistance of his body, then the roll of his flesh as he shoved the pike hard and harder, grunting with exertion. He heard a gurgled cry. The boy knelt down, his left hand still holding the pike, his right moving across the warm body to untie the sword and gun. Under his fingers he felt a twitch. His heart jumped. The thing still had life. He did not know how to load or shoot a gun, so he stood up, holding the Manchu running dog's sword high in the air. His arm was trembling from the weight of it. Despite the cold and rain, sweat broke out all over his body. "Think of a chicken," he told himself. "It is nothing but a Manchu cur. It is a demon opposing the will of Heaven." But his hand was high and still trembling, trembling. He remembered his pet dog cringing against the wall of the hut as his father stood over it with a cleaver. His father's arm had trembled as well.

Suddenly, a strong hand closed over his own. The sword came down with tremendous force. He thought he could hear the head rolling down the mountain, bouncing against the rocks.

"See," Chu was saying, "do not hesitate." His right hand remained on Wang Lee's. "It must be done quickly, without thought." He removed his hand and patted Wang Lee on the back. "The first time is always hard. Lay down your heart, little brother."

He helped the boy to strip the body. The soldier had a flintlock with powder, plug, and ammunition. Wang Lee kept putting his hand into warm blood. He wanted to scream or retch. He spit instead. Finally, the ghoulish task was done. Chu helped him roll the body off the pass into the wild where the vultures and beasts would dispose of it. The rebels wiped their swords and pikes and hands on the brown winter grass and headed back singing to their cave.

Chu was right. The task must be done without hesitation, and it did become easier. For a while, Wang Lee kept count of the demons he slew, but by spring, among the wild flowers and sweet new grass of the mountains, he did not bother to count. Most of the killing was at night. He remembered the first time he killed by day. That was a hard one. He saw the boy's face — a farm boy like himself with an old childhood scar, a white crescent, under his left eye. He wore his peasant dress rather than a uniform. Had he been kidnapped from his father's fields to be a soldier? They looked each other full in the face across a space of two hoes laid end to end. The boy mouthed the word *mercy*, but no orders had been given to spare demons, however young or seeking surrender. Wang Lee's flintlock, which he had learned to use well, was loaded and cocked, and so he shot the boy. Cleanly. He was proud of that. It was a clean, simple death. He could not, however, seem to break the habit of spitting against the spirits of those he killed.

More government troops were pouring into the area around Thistle Mountain. No one in Peking was laughing about the long-haired God-worshipers anymore. They were the Taiping rebels, and the best troops in the Imperial army were sent to wipe them off the mountain. But the best troops in the Imperial army did what they always did. They pillaged and raped and burned, and drove the farmers of four districts into the arms of the Taiping. No one, not even Feng at the height of his preaching, had won more converts for the Heavenly Kingdom than the government troops sent to destroy them.

It was among the new recruits that Wang Lee found his second teacher. He was a former country schoolmaster, and his name was Shen. He was entrusted to Wang Lee for indoctrination, for by now the boy was considered one of the old rebels. Shen, who was at least ten years older than Wang Lee, had been baptized by one of the long-noses in the Jesus people church in Canton. He himself owned a copy of the Holy Book, which only the kings of the Taiping were able to obtain. He let Wang Lee read from it for a while every day. He taught him hundreds of new characters and told him stories from the old Classics, because he was a scholar in the traditional style. Wang Lee, in turn, taught Shen all the rules and hymns and declarations that Mei Lin had struggled so to teach him.

Shen had lived with the long-noses in Canton, and he was not the least afraid of them. The Jesus long-noses, he said, were a little stupid and smelled horribly of red meat, but they were not unkind and certainly, whatever the rumors, did not steal babies and eat their eyeballs.

"Can they read and write?" asked Wang Lee.

"Hardly at all," said Shen. "I heard one long-nose, who was a teacher in his own land, complain that Chinese writing was no more than chicken scratches. And he was looking at a poem on a Han scroll."

Wang Lee tried to act shocked. Actually, he was delighted. How superior he felt to those once fearsome creatures. He could read and write what to them were chicken scratches. The ignorant pigs. And evil as well. He smiled at Shen. The time would come when they would enlighten the long-nose barbarians.

By late spring, troops and weaponry had grown to the point that the Taiping dared to leave the mountains and attack the government-held towns at its base. They captured Hsiang-chou in May with the constant aid of their enemies. The two generals of the Imperial forces were jealous of each other, it seemed. When one general launched an offensive against the rebels, the other would refuse to support it. Meantime, the soldiers of both generals harassed the peasants so, that more and more rushed to join the Taiping.

Despite their ineptitude, the Imperialists continued to possess numbers and firepower. More by blundering force than with skill, they managed to push the Taiping out of Hsiang-chou and, for a time, to surround their main fighting body. It was July, steaming and suffocating on the Kwangsi plain. As far as the government troops were concerned, it was far too hot to fight. The Taiping, low on ammunition, hesitated to try to break through the loose and lazy government lines.

One Sabbath they were called to assemble. The sun was blazing above. Wang Lee felt faint as he stood there, wondering why they were meeting thus in an enormous gathering instead of in their units for Sabbath worship. He could find neither Shen nor Chu, although he craned his neck about looking for them. The hymns began, and then the prayers, and then, instead of the usual preaching about Heavenly beliefs and behavior, Yang and Hsiao stood before them — small, wiry Yang and large, muscled Hsiao. They reminded the boy of traveling actors preparing for a show in the market square, except that they were so quiet, staring intensely out into the crowd. It made the boy want to look away, but he knew he must not. No one in the vast assembly made a sound or movement, not even to wipe the sweat from his face.

Then, suddenly, the two kings fell to the ground. Wang Lee rose on his tiptoes to see what was happening. He had seen an afflicted child in the market village do the same, his mouth white with foam, his body thrashing about, but to see two kings of the Taiping do so was a fearful sight. A cry came from the mouth of Yang — not his own scratchy voice, but a strange, shrill, birdcall of a sound.

"It is I!" The voice pierced Wang Lee's very heart. "I, the Heavenly Father, descended to earth this day with your Heavenly Elder Brother. My children, you have come to a season of testing. The demons surround you and threaten you. But do not lose heart. I, the Heavenly Father, the Sovereign High Emperor, am your Creator and Savior. Fight the demons. Subdue the earth."

Then came a second peculiar voice, this one from the mouth of Hsiao as he lay beating the earth with his arms and legs. "I am Jesus, the Elder Brother, descended to earth this day. Respect the word of the Heavenly Father. Obey the kings. Fight with a single heart, and I and the Heavenly Father will continue to dwell among you and speak to you."

At first the assembly was stunned. Then a single shout went up. "God be adored!"

There was a roar in reply. "God be adored!"

For a few seconds, Wang Lee listened to the repeated cry. He resisted being carried away by it, but there was no Shen or Chu or Mei Lin to turn to. He let go, and the words burst joyfully from the prison of his mind. He was screaming them over and over again. All the silly talk he had once despised... it was true. Here was the proof. The High God spoke directly to them. He was no idol of mud or stone. He was a power greater than thunder, and He had chosen *him*. Wang Lee never need fear again. God be adored!

As soon as the weather changed and the rains came, the Taiping broke through the enemy lines with enormous boldness. They sang as they marched, shouted as they fought. Their goal was the city of Yung-an about one hundred eighty li northeast of Thistle Mountain. There was no wealth in the city. The people were impoverished. But the poor had enriched the Taiping from its earliest days. In addition, Yung-an was surrounded by hills, and the Taiping knew how to fight in the hills.

They marched straight for the city, daring the Imperialists to follow. And the demons did follow, their uniforms sodden, the gunpowder as heavy as mud. The rain was relentless. It beat their heads, it turned the dust into mire, which sucked at their sandaled feet. At last the order to turn back was given. The Imperialists sighed with relief and bent their backs to climb the hill they had just descended.

Wang Lee was fiercely proud of Feng for knowing what those stupid Manchu would do even before they knew themselves. "They will turn," Feng said, "as soon as they realize that the gunpowder is useless. And we will be hidden in the hills, waiting." Wang Lee could hear the *slap, slap* of their feet better than he could see them come. He waited behind his bush, pike in hand. The gunpowder was too wet to use, but he did not care; the demons' gunpowder would be wet as well, and they had no pikes.

Yang had taken most of the Taiping Army and marched noisily into Yung-an, but Feng and Hsiao had picked their best men for the ambush. And he, Wang Lee, was one of the best. He no longer fought just to save his own life. He fought for the Heavenly Kingdom. It was like wrapping his body in metal armor and filling his heart and liver with the spirit of God.

He did not know how many demons he killed that night. His arm no longer trembled under the weight of the sword. The eyes of the dead no longer stared at him when he tried to fall asleep. He was more concerned with the amount of weaponry collected than the smell of blood upon his clothes. Sometimes he even forgot to spit.

At the celebration of victory in Yung-an the next day, he saw Mei Lin. She came toward him after the time of sacrifice with a half smile on her face, as though she were opening her mouth to greet him. Just then Shen walked up and handed him a cup of tea. He nodded thanks over the rim of the cup at him, turning quickly as he did so to go back to where his fellow soldiers had gathered. His long sword felt cold and comforting along his thigh. It would not look good for him if he appeared to be talking to a woman. He had just been promoted to sergeant and must set a spotless example. His heart must be single.

## CHAPTER ELEVEN
# HORSEWOMEN
## OF GOD

AT SUNSET on the first day of the New Age, when the feasting was done, Mei Lin had gathered up her meager possessions, bowed a farewell to Chu and the boy, and walked quickly in a southwesterly direction toward the area that had been designated as the women's camp. She held her head high and ignored the murmurs around her, indicating that wives were parting from husbands, sisters from brothers, parents from children. Partings must be borne. It was to be only for a little while — just until they took Nanking. And besides, she had no father or brother or son, no one who would miss her with a tender longing — except dear old Chu. God have mercy on him. As for the boy, he might be glad to be free of her.

In the middle of the path, a woman was embracing a boy of about twelve. "Oh, my heart and liver," she was saying, "bring honor to your mother."

Mei Lin almost stopped to reprimand the woman, but walked around them instead. Who had been this woman's teacher? Didn't she understand that honor was due only to the Sovereign High God? Yes. It was better that she, Mei Lin, was free from all human entanglements. Of course it was harder for these foolish women used to serving husbands and glorying in the birth and growth of sons. But they would learn. Surely that would be the chief benefit of a separate women's camp. These family-bound creatures would be able to see themselves as children of the Heavenly Father and sisters together, not just as servants to their husbands and sons.

And yet, why was her heart so chilled? Since the day she went to be a slave in the militia barracks, she had not walked so alone.

Mei Lin, though only eighteen, was one of the few experienced women warriors. She had also been of the company of God-worshipers for three full years, so she was elevated to a high position among the women. She was sent at once to the cave at the foot of Thistle Mountain, where the Heavenly King's own sister, Hsuan-chiao, had her headquarters. Hsuan-chiao was married to Hsiao, the Western King, through whom the Elder Brother Jesus himself came down to earth.

The first thing Mei Lin noticed when ushered into the presence of the Commander of All the Women was Hsuan-chiao's clothes. Mei Lin herself wore the faded blue clothes of a peasant — tunic, trousers, and sash of coarse Nanking cotton. Her only color was the red kerchief that she wore as a turban on her hair.

The woman seated on a stool inside the mountain cave wore silk. The silk was yellow, a long court robe over a full skirt, which didn't quite cover her large Hakka feet. On the robe was embroidered the single phoenix and dragon of her husband, the Western King. A yellow silk turban was wound about her head. She was young and handsome in the broad-faced Hakka way, but there was something in the face that made Mei Lin duck her head into a bow. She had the feeling she remembered when summoned by the first wife of the master.

"I don't suppose you embroider," were the commander's first words.

"This humble person has been a spy and a foot soldier." Mei Lin had fallen back into the polite forms of her days as a servant. "Her fingers are, alas, too rough for a needle and silk."

"Yes. I can see that. Well, sit down. At least your feet are big. So many of the new recruits have lily-feet and will be useless in battle."

Mei Lin sat. There was no stool brought for her, so she sat down cross-legged on the earthen floor of the cave.

"They tell me you have the rank of captain."

"My elder sister has been correctly informed." Later Mei Lin learned that Hsuan-chiao preferred the title "commander" to the more familiar "sister," but she sensed, even now, that a greater show of respect was demanded. She kept her head bowed and did not look again at the woman's face.

"My husband, who by the appointment of God is the Western King, has sent to me his younger sister San-niang. Our younger sister has asked that you serve as her adjutant." The Commander of All the Women swept her hand to the right, and a tall young woman, dressed like Mei Lin in the clothes of a peasant, stepped from a shadowy corner of the cave and came and sat down near Mei Lin. The resemblance between her and the Western King was apparent, though in the lamplight Mei Lin saw a gentleness that she had never seen in the face of the king.

"You do not shoot with a bow," San-niang said rather than asked.

"No. I have no such skill," Mei Lin answered.

"You do not ride a horse."

"No." Perhaps San-niang would not want her after all. Her heart sank.

"They tell me you saved the life of the Southern King, that you were a spy as far north as Kweilin, and that you fought valiantly in the most recent campaign."

"This humble person seeks to serve the Heavenly Kingdom as she can." Mei Lin did not dare look into San-niang's face, for fear she would seem to be begging to be chosen.

"Good. I can teach you to ride and shoot properly." San-niang turned and bowed to Hsuan-chiao. "She is exactly the person I want. Brave and teachable."

And so began a new chapter in Mei Lin's life. First, San-niang taught her archery. San-niang herself could shoot with either arm. It was a skill regarded by the enemy as a kind of witchcraft. She did not demand this extraordinary ability from others and was quite satisfied when Mei Lin became proficient with the right arm only. To San-niang, the bow was the best of all weapons: quiet and deadly, and easily reloaded on horseback.

San-niang chose five others beside Mei Lin from the experienced women soldiers. She took them up into the wilds of Thistle Mountain while there was still snow on the upper slopes. As the daughter of a charcoal bearer, she had grown up on the mountain. She knew where the springs were and which roots to dig for food or medicine. The women learned to kill mouse deer and rabbits, even field mice on the run, and to retrieve every arrow. They called one another sister, but they became more like one person, so well did they understand one another's needs and wishes. San-niang was truly a part of the whole. "We are born of the same Heavenly Father," she would say. "We are the same bone and flesh."

Word came up to them that the Imperial troops were marching upon Chin-t'ien and that the whole body of the Taiping was being ordered to the mountain. "It is time to join the rest," San-niang said. They went back quickly to the women's camp and helped the others move into the mountains. Then San-niang chose twenty-five other young women. She gave each of her sisters the charge of five women to train for warfare, except Mei Lin, whom she kept to be her adjutant. Gradually, each new recruit was sent to enlist five more under herself, so that when the fierce mountain fighting began, San-niang's army had grown to a hundred twenty-five women. They shot from behind pine trees or bushes with deadly accuracy. As spring came, they left off their cloth shoes, which had been ruined by snow and mud, and scrambled barefoot over the rocks.

With spring, too, came the horses. San-niang's had been hidden in a valley on the southeast side of the mountain. One clear April day, she took Mei Lin with her to fetch it and, at the same time, to choose a horse for her adjutant.

On horseback, San-niang looked like a warrior goddess of the ancient stories. Her long black hair streamed out behind her like a banner as she rode. There was no saddle, only two narrow strips of rein. San-niang let these lie across her hand, barely holding them at all. "We must command with our bodies," she explained. "Our hands must be free for the bow." Back and forth through the length of the narrow gorge she rode. Mei Lin, watching her diminish into the distance, held her breath. Somehow she feared that the tiny horse and rider might, on reaching the farther end, take off into the sky like an eagle soaring high over the mountains, never to return. But each time, the figure — the horse and woman were one being, there at the limit of her vision — would arc until now it was flying toward her, growing in size and power and loveliness as it came. "She is mortal just as I am. She is my barefoot sister from Thistle Mountain." Mei Lin pulled a piece of wild grass and sucked its bitter stem. It was the only thing that tasted of reality. The rest — the green spring valley with its delicate embroidery of flowers, the dark plum mountain overhead, the peacock sky, the rider whose blue garments faded in the sunlight to a dazzling white, the brownish red horse — was an enchantment. "God be adored." It was a whispered incantation against falling into a world other than the stern kingdom that was her sworn home.

"Now," said San-niang, bringing her horse at last to the place where Mei Lin stood. "My playtime is over. We have work to do." She called to one of the men who tended the horses. She asked for a mare, broken but not too meek. "She must not be afraid," San-niang said. "She will be a soldier as much as you."

The horse was small and shaggy, having been born and raised on the northwestern steppes beyond the Great Wall. With San-niang's hands under her right foot, Mei Lin swung easily to the back of the little beast. Next, San-niang put Mei Lin's hands on the reins, just so. Then, with her own hands, she molded Mei Lin's legs to the body of the horse. Mei Lin could feel the warmth of the creature's body through her legs and thighs, from toe to toe, as though both of them were naked. She was hardly used to this strange physical comfort when, at San-niang's command, the animal plunged forward, and Mei Lin began to bounce brutally against not flesh and blood but a body of steel. The reins flew from her hand. She grabbed forward for the mane, but failing to reach it, slid off the side of the beast onto the grass. San-niang came running, laughing as she did so. The little horse was waiting a few steps ahead, swishing her tail and stomping her feet impatiently. Probably laughing, too, the brute.

Once again, San-niang put her on the horse's back and molded her body to the curve of the animal's back. And again. And again. By the end of the day, Mei Lin was more bruised than a fallen persimmon, but she was riding. There was no divinity about her form, but she was no longer falling off. They had no time for further practice. The next day she had to put her flesh, stiff and purple, upon the back of the horse one more time, and head across the mountain for the Taiping camp.

Horses could not be used for mountain fighting. But when there was a lull, San-niang and Mei Lin rode and taught others to ride. Again they increased their army by a multiple of five, so that when, with the end of the spring, the Taiping were ready to move down from the mountain and carry the fighting onto the plains and into the river valleys, San-niang's army numbered more than six hundred big-footed women, of which a hundred were on horseback.

The horsewomen were not needed for the battle of Yung-an. The rain was such a formidable ally that they were never called up; but they knew they were ready. Mei Lin prayed daily that she would not fall to the sin of pride, but surely the High God himself took a fierce joy in His horsewomen.

She saw Wang Lee at the sacrifices in celebration of the capture of Yung-an. All the Taiping were gathered in the city by then, women and children as well as men. The smoke hardly rose. The smell of burning dog flesh hung strong and sickening in the heavy air. He was standing near an altar that had been hastily erected with broken bricks. His hair flowed down across his shoulders. It had been carefully washed and combed, and it gleamed like a woman's. He wore a sergeant's insignia, a rhinoceros emblem on the front of his tunic. He was taller than she remembered, and broader through the shoulders. His face no longer relaxed into the slack expression of the ignorant pigboy she had known. The eyes now were glittering, the mouth tight. How proud he was! Even when he was nothing more than a stupid peasant child, arrogance had been his greatest temptation. And now... Ah, well, he was still young. Perhaps when he had wrestled a bit longer with life... She started across the short distance toward him, but he turned, pretending not to have seen her. She smiled to herself. The little rhinoceros sergeant would not know, at least not for a while, that he had just turned his back on a leopard colonel.

## CHAPTER TWELVE
# SHEN

THE DAY AFTER the celebration, Wang Lee and Shen were taking a walk around the top of the wall. It was damp and drizzly, but not actually raining, and there was no enemy in sight.

"Who was she?" Shen asked.

"Who was who?" Wang Lee feigned ignorance. He didn't want of talk of Mei Lin, certainly not to Shen.

"The young woman yesterday. The leopard colonel."

"Oh, yes." Why hadn't he noticed that she'd been promoted? "The sister who, with Old Chu, brought me into the Kingdom."

"But you didn't speak to her."

He felt his face prickling with discomfort. "She is a woman. I must set an example for my men."

"You are forbidden to greet your spiritual teacher?"

"I thought it best..." He wanted to sound dignified for Shen, who was his pupil. It amazed Wang Lee that the man, a scholar and a teacher in his own right, came quite humbly to him to be taught. He who knew the Classics as well as the teachings of the Jesus people was still a searcher for Truth. He had a way of pointing his right index finger heavenward just an inch or so from his nose, shaking it ever so slightly as he spoke. His left hand invariably held a book or a pamphlet. Sometimes the finger would dive to the text like a cormorant to a fish, catching the appropriate passage and holding it while he read aloud. It seemed to Wang Lee the gesturing of a true scholar. Sometimes as the boy lay in his quilt, going over the happenings of the day, he would practice shaking his finger beside his nose and swooping it down to an imaginary book. When the campaign was over and he himself became a scholar, he would hold his finger just so as he taught, ready at any moment to stab the book from which he expounded wisdom.

In the meantime, he would learn from Shen, as well as teach him. The two of them took watch together whenever possible. One day Shen asked if he might move into the house where Wang Lee and his men were quartered, so that they could study in their free moments. "There is so much about the Heavenly Kingdom that I do not understand," he said.

Wang Lee found it increasingly harder to teach Shen. Who could have imagined such questions?

"If then," Shen asked, "Jesus is the Elder Son and the Heavenly King the Younger Son of the High God, do they have the same or different mothers?"

Wang Lee's head felt like a rock. He'd never thought of Heavenly Mothers.

Shen's forefinger went beside his nose. "Perhaps it is a matter of spiritual fatherhood and not fatherhood of the flesh?"

"Perhaps. Yes, perhaps so."

"If Yang is, as it is said, the Holy Ghost, and it is through him that the High God descends to earth, why don't we revere him more than we do the Heavenly King, who is but the Younger Son of the High God?"

The rock head was beginning to spin. "It is all explained," Wang Lee said, "in the declarations. It is all clear there. But I am nothing but an ignorant peasant, I've only just learned to read.... If only Feng could teach you."

"No, no," Shen insisted. "You are a fine teacher. It is that my mind has been muddled with false doctrines." He would shake his head, his finger still poised beside his nose. "It is wrong of me to question."

And so it went through the fall. There was time for the struggle of the mind because war seemed far away. The government troops had withdrawn beyond the hills, and the Taiping could enjoy the protection of this great walled city, whose inhabitants treated them as saviors. "This is the easiest time of my old life," Chu said once. "Never before has my soul had time to catch up with my body."

Wang Lee felt a little smug. He had learned nearly a thousand characters in those three months.

It was a freezing morning early in the second year of the New Age. Wang Lee realized that someone was trying to shake him awake, but he tightened his body into a ball under the quilt, hating to stick even his nose out into the chilled morning. It was only Chu after all, wanting to take a walk to the marketplace, or some other foolishness. The old man persisted until the boy loosened his ears enough to hear what his old companion was saying. "Get up! Get up! The demons have come back!"

At this, Wang Lee swung off the platform into his cloth shoes before his eyes were fully open. "Where?"

"They are surrounding the walls. They have great guns, larger than water buffalo. Come, you can see clearly from the wall."

In the east, the first light burned a harsh crimson, like a grass fire low in the sky. On the hills just below there was movement — the scurrying of mice from a burning field, but not quite so fast. Despite what Chu said, Wang Lee could not see clearly, but he could see enough to know that many creatures were moving over the hills. "They come from every direction," Chu whispered, as though imparting secret information. Wang Lee shivered and stuck his hands up the opposite sleeves of his padded jacket and hugged his arms close. His breath was white in the gray light. Now he could see the guns, bearers pulling them with ropes, and even more men pulling from the side to keep the heavy artillery from rolling uncontrolled back down the hill.

"They have long-nose guns," Chu was saying. "One day the long-noses are killing the Manchu; the next they are selling them foreign-devil guns." He shook his head. "There are those who pretend to understand the long-noses, but this Chu is only a simple fellow."

"Shen will want to see this," Wang Lee said. "He knows all about these things." He turned from the wall to press through the crowd of Taiping who were now beginning to gather, and caught a parting glimpse of Chu, pinching the drip from his nose and shaking his head.

When the great devil guns were rolled in place and the wheels blocked with stones, the bombardment began. The Imperial troops, fearing, it seemed, the marksmanship of the rebel archers, had been reluctant to bring the guns in close enough to do real damage. The rebels standing atop the wall had the ideal place from which to watch the show. Below, the squirrel-sized Imperialists loaded the cannonballs, fired the powder, and jumped back as the balls went hurtling toward the wall at tremendous speed, only to plop harmlessly to the earth several yards away from the target.

"They'll have to bring the silly cannon in closer," Shen said.

"Ah, and you are the demons' general?" Wang Lee asked.

Shen looked at him quickly.

Wang Lee flushed. "You'd be better than the ones they have," the boy said.

Shen relaxed. It had been a joke.

The guns were brought in closer, their wheels blocked again. This time the bombardment ceased to be quite so much a game. The balls began to hit the wall and, from time to time, to explode. Sometimes the cannons exploded, sending debris and cannoneers flying into the air, to loud cheers from the wall. But the fun was clearly at an end. The commanders set a rotation for guarding the wall, and all the troops remained on constant alert.

Now that the times of study were limited, they were more precious than ever to Wang Lee. He hardly bothered to instruct Shen anymore, so eager was he to learn all that his friend could teach him. Shen told him stories of the heroes from the Holy Book. Wang Lee especially liked the king named David, who slew giants with pebbles and established a great throne with the help of the High God. He did not like the part when David fell to the sin of adultery, but it was, as Shen said, a helpful teaching. Shen also told him tales of Chinese heroes. Wang Lee had heard some of the stories before, of course, from traveling storytellers and players in the market town, but Shen was a better reciter than any he had ever heard.

One unfamiliar poem caught like a hook in the boy's head. It was a war poem. They were never without the sound of war now. Even in the safety of their little mud house, they could hear the cannons. Shen read the poem from one of his books, his forefinger holding the place:

> *Men die in the field, slashing sword to sword.*
> *The horses of the conquered neigh piteously*
> *    to Heaven.*
> *Crows and hawks peck for human guts,*
> *Carry them in their beaks and hang them on*
> *    the branches of withered trees.*
> *Captains and soldiers are smeared on the bushes*
> *    and grass;*
> *The General schemed in vain.*
> *Know therefore that the sword is a cursed thing*
> *Which the wise man uses only if he must.*

Wang Lee reached for his padded jacket and put it on against the sudden coldness of the room. "That is also the teaching of the Heavenly Kingdom," he said at last.

Shen looked up from the book, but he left his finger on the place.

"Hasn't the Heavenly King said, 'What a pity that men should kill each other'?" Wang Lee went on.

"Yes," said Shen.

They were together on the wall that bright, bright, bitter February day, when one of the cannon-balls did reach its target. Wang Lee watched in fascination. It seemed to be coming straight toward them. Soon it would drop, and they would cheer... and perhaps sing. He was actually choosing the hymn when Shen cried out and threw him from behind to knock him clear of the explosion. He was hardly hurt. Just a sliver of shrapnel in his right hip. The barber was fetched, and he removed the metal in a few minutes.

"Good," said Shen. "It is nothing, after all."

How could it be nothing? One of Wang Lee's privates was now dead. Wang Lee had seen men die before, but that had been different. None of those men had belonged to him. None of them was under his care and protection. But today, while he was picking out a hymn, a charcoal bearer who had eaten nothing but bitterness for most of the short span of his life was struck in the chest with a large shard of devil shrapnel. The man died slowly, screaming out to Heaven. If Wang Lee had been more careful, if he had been less interested in Shen and the flattering task of being a teacher to a scholar, of becoming a scholar himself when his duty was to be a soldier...

The private's body was put in a sturdy coffin and covered with lime. It could not be buried as long as the city was under siege. At the celebration of his death, Wang Lee, as the man's sergeant, had to preside. According to the doctrines, death was a lucky event. Was not the soul of his brother even now with the Heavenly Father in Paradise? "We do not mourn," Wang Lee instructed the others. "We rejoice on this happy occasion." But the funeral words stuck in his throat, and he had to force them out. He did not begrudge his brother's entrance into

Heaven, but he bore on his own body the weight of this unnecessary death.

For three days he mourned in secret. He kept his face unlined and his hair carefully combed. No one was to know of his shame. But Shen must have suspected. The man did not speak of it directly. He was too much of a gentleman. But he began to hint that a leech had fastened itself on Wang Lee's soul.

Wang Lee kept his peace. It would be ungrateful to complain to the very man who had saved his own miserable life that his action had not been enough. Yet why had Shen saved him for a life of remorse?

The bombardment grew heavier. Even deep in the midst of the city in their one-room house, the *thud, thud, thud* of the cannonry punctuated their very breathing. Shen had his head cocked, listening. Wang Lee studied the thin face, as beautifully carved as a piece of sandalwood, wondering at all the elegant thoughts crowded behind those eyes. He was not prepared for the words that came out.

"More will die tonight," Shen was saying.

"Lucky are they who enter Paradise wearing the emblem of Great Peace." Wang Lee was glad to have so much memorized. Words would roll off his tongue unbidden, leaving the bitter core hidden in his heart.

"The Imperial forces are growing stronger by the day."

"In the end, the demons will all perish."

Shen smiled. "Those poor sons of turtles are hardly demons...."

"He who is a running dog of the Manchu emperor…"

"They're just poor Han Chinese like ourselves — kidnapped or impressed or sold by their starving fathers into service.…"

He knew Shen was right, but it was like the sip of disloyalty that Chu had once warned against. He was glad they were alone in the house.

"We should not be killing them, nor they us," Shen went on.

"We did not begin the killing," Wang Lee said stubbornly.

"'Under Heaven all men are brothers.'" Shen began to quote back the very words Wang Lee had taught him. "'Their souls all come from Heaven; in the eyes of the High God they are all his sons. What a pity that men should kill each other.'"

Wang Lee was silent. There was something about Shen's voice that frightened him. Surely it was not the words. They were more familiar to him now than his own never spoken name. No, it was not the words themselves, it was the way Shen invoked them that made Wang Lee take his heart into his hand.

They were both silent, staring at the sputtering wick swimming in its rough earthenware dish of peanut oil. The low light gave Shen's face a ghostly glow. At last he began to speak. He was telling one of the ancient stories. Wang Lee knew that there would be a teaching folded into the tale.

"It is said" — Shen half closed his eyes and leaned back on the stool to rest against the mud wall — "it is said that once the teacher Confucius saw a woman weeping beside a roadside tomb. He sent one of his disciples to ask the woman the cause of her grief.

"'You weep,' the disciple said to the woman, 'as though you had eaten nothing but bitterness in this world.'

"'You speak rightly,' answered the woman. 'In this world I have borne sorrow upon sorrow. At this very spot my father-in-law was killed by a tiger, and then my husband also. And now my only son is dead, killed by the tiger as well.'

"'Why then, do you not leave this unlucky place?' he asked.

"'Because,' she answered, 'here in this place there is no tyrannical government.'

"And Confucius turned to his disciples and said to them: 'My children, oppressive government is fiercer than a tiger. Remember this.'"

A great wave of relief washed over Wang Lee's body. The oppressive government could only be that of the Manchu conquerors. He lay down his heart and began to breathe evenly. But only for a moment, because Shen was not finished.

He spoke, his voice cold as a sword blade on a winter night. "I could not even get wine or opium for your dying private."

"Wine and opium are forbidden."

"Yes." Shen leaned over the table and blew out the wick. "And tigers."

They curled up under their quilts on the platform bed without speaking to each other again. The evening prayers had gone unsaid. Wang Lee did not know when the others would return, so he recited the prayers in his head. He had sung songs of rejoicing at the death of his private. What hymns were sung for the death of friendship?

He was very clever. Shen must not guess his suspicions. He never spoke until the two of them were alone, and nearly always he played the role of pupil.

"What does the Holy Book teach us about the Manchu demons?"

"The Holy Book does not speak of the Manchu." The finger went up. It seemed more and more a womanish gesture, unbecoming to a soldier. "You see, the Holy Book was written many years ago, but it does say... Here..." He found and punched the place. "'Submit yourselves to every government of man for the High God's sake, whether it be to the king as supreme, or unto governors, or...'"

"But the Manchu stole the dragon throne. They are not Han Chinese. They are nomad dogs."

"Even in the Holy Book there are foreign conquerors."

"But hasn't the High God given to our Heavenly King the Mandate of Heaven?"

"The Mandate of Heaven is a teaching of Confucius. It does not appear in the Holy Book."

"But surely the Holy Book says that the Heavenly Kingdom on earth will begin here in the Middle Kingdom. China is chosen by God, is it not?"

"I cannot find it written."

"Then" — his face hidden in the shadows, he whispered now — "then what are we to do?"

"Ah," said Shen, "what indeed?"

A farmer plants and waits for harvest. Wang Lee could wait. It was his task in the Heavenly Kingdom to learn infinite patience. He did not stir. He hardly breathed as he waited. The words must come from Shen's own mouth.

Several days passed, but then one night the scholar said it. "If those of us of like mind would band together... we could slip a man over the wall. We could send word that some of us wish to stop the killing."

"Ah." Wang Lee permitted himself the single syllable.

"Why should Han Chinese kill one another at the command of a Manchu on one side and a Hakka on the other?"

"It is too heavy for my simple mind," Wang Lee said in his old peasant manner.

The men came in, prayers were said. Wang Lee lay awake, listening to the noises of sleep. He did not know if Shen were awake as well, making his own plans. But he must no longer think of Shen as brother; he must not remember that Shen had saved his life. The Heavenly Kingdom was greater than any feelings and obligations of a single soldier. A viper had stolen into the camp. That was what he must remember.

He waited. Shen must not guess anything. He waited for one of those rare occasions when Shen and the new recruits were sent to guard the wall and he and his men were not. Then he went directly to the headquarters of the Tung Wang. Yang, as prime minister, commander-in-chief, and Eastern King, was also in charge of security. Wang Lee gave his report to the captain on duty.

The boy was not sure what he expected to happen, and at first nothing happened at all. The bombardment continued and increased in strength and accuracy. Patrols on the wall were doubled. The enemy were in arrow and firing range now, and sharpshooters and marksmen picked off cannoneers all day long. More came to take their places. The attack had gone on for over a month, and the Taiping knew that they had halted the Imperial army with its long-nose guns. Morale was high, and the kings intended to keep it high. Lists were posted every few days, with the names of those who were to be promoted or honored. Declarations were written and printed and thrown from the walls: *Behold, you multitudes, and listen to our words. We believe that the empire belongs to the Chinese and not to the Manchu....*

Rewards were offered to any who would desert the Imperial troops and join the Taiping, and those who had already done so within the city were summoned to the presence of the kings for their rewards.

One day Shen's name appeared on the list of new recruits to be honored. He bathed carefully and dressed in clean garments. He combed his long hair until it shone, and tied a turban about it as though ready for battle. Then he went to meet the kings.

He did not return in time for supper. Wang Lee was squatting with his men by the small charcoal burner outside the house, eating the last of his rice, when Chu suddenly appeared.

"Have you eaten yet, elder brother?" Wang Lee asked.

Chu pushed aside the polite phrase and came to squat down beside him. "God be adored," he said quietly, so the others could not hear. "You are safe."

"What is it?" Every hair on Wang Lee's body seemed to stand up separately like the hairs on a dog's back when it is threatened.

"God descended to earth today."

Wang Lee's chopsticks rattled against the side of his empty bowl. He put them down to hide his shaking hand.

"Shen was called forward to receive his reward. But just then, the Tung Wang was seized by the Spirit of God, who cried out that Shen was a spy and an enemy of the High God. My hand was in my heart with fear for my little brother. You and the traitor..."

"Lay down your heart, elder brother," he said, hoping that Chu could not hear the quaver. "The High God knows I am not a traitor." But his own heart went out of his body.

Yang's men came and fetched Shen's books and possessions. Wang Lee could not make himself go to the trial. He had a frozen dread that he might be called as a witness, but he was never summoned. Instead, the High God himself was the witness, coming to earth through the Tung Wang to accuse and give details of Shen's treachery. The traitor's handsome turbaned head was parted swiftly from his body and placed on a pike over the east gate of the city. Wang Lee took care not to see it, but it came to him in dreams, all the same. The eyes were wide open, staring at his face, and the lips were parted as if in speech. The hair was brown and matted with blood, and sometimes there would be a single finger shaking slightly beside the nose. The boy would wake with a lurch and lean over to spit on the earth floor.

## CHAPTER THIRTEEN

# The Destruction
# of Chuan-chou

THE ATTACK had been brought to a standstill, but the enemy remained encircled about Yung-an. The Taiping were not afraid of the cannons or of the men behind them, but as weeks dragged on, they began to fear a more powerful enemy — the specter Want. And so it was decided in the council of the kings that the siege must be broken before hunger and lack of ammunition were allowed to do what the Manchu could not. The Taiping did not wait for lucky days. Feng had taught them that the Heavenly Father created all days, so no day could be called unlucky. But they did wait for one gift from Heaven — rain. The great teacher Experience had taught them that they who worshiped God could fight in any weather, but the Imperial troops lost courage in the rain.

It rained all day on the fifth of April, continuing into the night. There was no moon to reveal the silent opening of the great north gate or the line of men slipping one by one through the crack. The first objective was the gunpowder wagons. The Taiping struck swiftly and quietly, before the Imperial troops came fully awake. With the capture of the wagons, more rebels poured out of the gate to protect those who were dragging the wagons back toward the city.

Wang Lee and his men waited behind the city walls for orders. They were under Feng, and thus not in the vanguard that Yang commanded and that had left the protection of the city hours before. At last dawn came, and with it the order to move. They were sent not out of the gate but to the top of the wall, to protect the rear of Yang's army from above. Wang Lee shook off his disappointment and shouted to his men, now only three. They joined Chu's unit and climbed the stone staircase up to the north wall. Morning was nothing that day but a gradual lightening of the sky from ebony to steel.

When it was light enough to join the battle, Wang Lee hesitated to give the order. The scene below was a tangle of men struggling body to body. How could one shoot and not hit a brother? "Wait," he told his impatient men, "wait. When they turn to flee, then shoot."

He stayed in the niche of the wall, his flintlock pressed against his shoulder, his eyes squinted. He hardly dared stretch or blink for fear he would miss the single opportune moment. Men were dying down below. Even now Shen's eyes were staring at the dead from over the east gate — unless the crows had already plucked his eyes from their sockets.

A great shout came from below. At first he could not make out the words. He saw, however, that the gate had opened once again, and streaming out from it in a flood of color and speed and power were the horsewomen of San-niang. He could recognize San-niang even from that height and distance. She controlled her horse entirely with her knees and legs, and shot as she rode, switching her bow from one hand to the other as the target demanded. She was soon only a yellow dot at the head of her hundred horsewomen, their hair streaming out from under their yellow turbans, their bows a black line against their yellow tunics, their skirts blood red on the backs of their shaggy beasts. The horsewomen were followed by hundreds of brightly dressed women foot soldiers running behind the cavalry, shouting as they went.

The Taiping had been warned, so at the first cry of "The women!" they leapt or ran or rolled out of the path of the horses. But the startled government troops first stopped to stare openmouthed at the apparition, and then, too late, turned and ran away from the female ghosts who galloped down upon them.

Chu was smiling like a laughing buddha. "Did you see her?" he shouted at Wang Lee over the din. The boy thought the old man meant San-niang, so he nodded and smiled back. "She was never on a horse before last spring. Now she's a woman warrior from the old tales!"

Something like disappointment pricked Wang Lee. The old man meant Mei Lin. She had passed through on that terrible wave of beauty and power, and he had not known to look for her.

He could not dwell on it. Their orders had come. While the women created confusion at the north side, Feng's men were to travel swiftly out the east gate to a place called the cliffs of Lung-liao. They were to wait there for the fleeing army. They did their job well. Nearly five thousand government soldiers perished at the cliffs. The siege of Yung-an was broken.

Now the Taiping would go on to Kweilin, leaving two thousand of their own behind and the desiccated head of Shen still guarding the east gate.

The route to Kweilin was a tortuous one. They had to abandon all the captured cannons. There was no way to pull them through the narrow passes and across the mountains. Frequently Wang Lee and his men stepped off the path to let horses go past. Each time he heard the sound of hoofs, he wondered if it might be Mei Lin; but he never saw her during the eleven-day march. It was, in truth, more of a creep than a march. They had to remain in the protecting cleft of the mountains, and there were many wounded who could not climb unassisted. And, as always, there were the old and weak, the children, and the lily-footed women who must also be carried. Had the world ever seen such a beggarly army? The Imperial forces knew no such handicaps.

They headed straight for the river, commandeered boats and boatmen, and arrived at Kweilin well before the rebels.

On the eighteenth day of April, the rebels began their attack. Now they were surrounding the city, and the Imperialists were defending it. But this time there was a great difference — the Taiping had no artillery. They could not, even after a month of siege, take the city. Reluctantly the Tung Wang gave the order to withdraw. The Taiping would leave the well-guarded, well-supplied city of Kweilin and march onto the broad plains of Hunan Province, where there was already great sympathy for their cause.

The enemy were behind the walls of Kweilin. The Taiping had little fear of attack as they began again the long journey, first to Changsha and then on toward Nanking.

Wang Lee found himself retracing his own journey of nearly two years before — through the ghostly Li valley, up to the canal hidden in the mountains, until they were marching beside the river that he had labored up that bitter summer before he met Mei Lin and Chu in the now closed city of Kweilin. He thought of his parents and wondered how they were faring and if the seed rice in the northeast corner of the wall had ever been planted. He did not allow himself to bathe in these concerns. It would not be worthy. The Heavenly Kingdom must occupy his every breath.

He had no sooner quieted his heart than he saw a sight that threw it to the winds like chaff from a threshing basket. As Feng's army re-formed their line for the march one morning, they went past the women's army of San-niang. At the front of her women, her figure straight as a man's, San-niang sat on the back of her brownish red horse, and close beside, on a little gray war-horse, was Mei Lin. Wang Lee might have missed seeing her, except that Chu elbowed him just at the moment before they passed by. Her face was dark as oiled wood and near-ly shone under the yellow silk turban. Her tunic, too, was yellow silk, embroidered with the leopard of a colonel, and her red silk riding skirt clung to the body of her mount. She had a bow slung across her right shoulder, the bowstring across her breast, and a quiver of arrows lashed to the back of her left shoulder. He could hardly see her feet, brown and bare, tucked into the sides of the horse. She was pat-ting its neck and talking to it while it waited impa-tiently, stamping its hoofs and tossing its shaggy mane. Her own hair fell across her shoulders as she leaned forward toward the horse's head. Suppose she did not see him at all? Or suppose she would refuse to acknowledge him? But as he and Chu drew just opposite, she turned her head, tossed her hair back over her shoulder, and looked at him. She did not smile, but she nodded first at Chu and then at him. For a moment he could not breathe. She had changed. He could not understand how, until they were past and Chu said between his teeth, "See how pretty she's got. Must be good food." Wang Lee knew it was more than food.

It took them nearly half the morning to re-form the line. It was the duty of Feng's men to secure wagons and wheelbarrows for those who needed assistance. The way was at last smooth enough for wheels. The weak would no longer have to be carried on the backs of the strong.

Wang Lee watched with Chu as the women with bound feet hobbled on their heels to the wagons or wheelbarrows assigned them, and he remembered Mei Lin climbing the mountain on her strong broad feet. How could he have thought them ugly? These stupid, crippled women would slow the Heavenly Kingdom to a snail's crawl. Even their faces looked bound and crippled. "How useless these creatures are," he said aloud.

"They sew," Chu said, "and make arrows. They do what they can."

Wang Lee did not complain again.

At last the women and the weak were all loaded. Feng ordered his men into their ranks, and then for a while he walked with them himself. When it was clear that all was in order and moving as well as possible, the Southern King climbed into his yellow sedan chair at the end of the column. He reminded Wang Lee of Mei Lin, quietly doing what must be done, never asking whether it lacked dignity.

The sedan chairs of the other kings were far ahead of his. Except when they needed a scholar, they ignored him. For writing declarations and waiting in ambush and serving as sheep dog for the weak of the flock, Feng was in demand. He was the one whom the people, the ordinary brothers and sisters, loved most of all. They believed not only that Feng understood everything but that he could make it clear to the simplest child. And yet the other kings put him at the end of the line.

Wang Lee could not hold the taste of bitterness for long. There was too much of a festive air about this journey. For the first time since early fall, they were free of threat from the Manchu. Spring had come to the river valley, and the dazzling green of the bamboo, five times taller than a man, crowded the opposite bank and danced in the breeze beside the towpath where the Taiping forces were strung out li after li. It was a wonderful season for walking. Wang Lee, remembering this journey as a struggle upstream with a towrope burning his shoulder, could hardly feel the weight of gun or pike or sword or supply bundle. There were no cities nearby whose offal might foul the river. The fresh smell of water and air and new green filled their lungs with power, and the rebels could not help but burst into song as they marched. It was a beautiful river, broad but shallow, so that the round bottom stones gleamed like freshly steamed meat rolls. They caught fish to cook with their rice, and garnished their bowls with bamboo shoots and roots from the woods.

Nearly a week had passed since the Taiping left Kweilin behind. The thick groves of bamboo gave way to cultivated fields. The first rice was high and green. To the west, under the shadow of the mountains, rose the walls of the city of Chuan-chou. They could see the sentries on its walls, but they had no fear of them. There were no Imperial troops quartered there, only a weak provincial militia. The city was not worth a single arrow. Yang ordered the Taiping to march by close enough so that their show of strength and their great numbers would impress the local officials. The local officials were impressed and watched with terror and then relief as the enormous army filed past.

But a country boy, conscripted not long before, stood in a niche above the east gate of the city. The longer he watched the rebel procession, the heavier his fowling piece weighed. After what seemed endless hours of watching, the end of the march came past him, and with it a single yellow sedan chair, the curtains rolled up to reveal a man also dressed in yellow. If he could kill a rebel king, what indeed would be his reward? He aimed the slender barrel at the yellow figure and pulled the trigger. The long gun jolted against his shoulder.

"Aieee! Aieee!" The cry went up from the chair bearers and spread through the miles of marchers and cavalry. "Feng! Feng! Feng!" they cried. "The demon shot Feng!"

The cry went through Wang Lee as though a pike had been driven through his belly. He watched, his body frozen, as the bearers laid the Southern King gently down upon the path. A doctor and a barber rushed to the spot while the bearers and members of Feng's personal guard pushed back the stricken crowd. Wang Lee could no longer see the king. He began to recite a prayer. It didn't seem to matter what prayer — any prayer would be one for Feng's life. Chu joined him. And then came the smell and presence of a horse. Mei Lin was above them.

"He is alive," she said, able to see over the heads of the crowd. "God be adored."

The order came to make camp. There was no place to stop except in the midst of the cultivated fields, but no one noted that they were breaking regulations. Commanders of the units made up of miners were called to the Tung Wang's tent. The High God had spoken to Yang. The Taiping were to tunnel under the walls of this accursed city. They must show its inhabitants the wrath of the Almighty God reserved for those who sought to destroy His kings.

That night there was no sleep or food. Instead, there were gatherings all over the fields around great bonfires. There was a frenzy of preparation and then the call to more meetings. The word of the High God, which had come down to Yang, was repeated over and over: "The enemies of the High God must be utterly destroyed!"

By morning the camp had settled to a quiet more terrifying than the screams and shouts of the night before. Morning prayers were recited and then each division was given its task. The horsewomen were to gallop about the walls, shooting arrows of fire into the city. Foot soldiers were to march around and around a hundred abreast, singing as loudly as they could. Blacksmiths would beat their hammers against the city gates. The clamor would cover the work of the miners, which was to tunnel under the walls.

Wang Lee rotated his men so that each would have an hour's rest after three hours of marching. He must have slept, but he could not remember having done so. His body was stretched taut, like a string drawn back on a powerful bow. His head hummed with the tension.

He must have eaten, but he could hardly remember that either. One night, they were marching under a ghost moon, their tight throats pinching the sound of their hymns until they were more shriek than music. Someone caught up with his line and pressed something round and warm into his hand. He never saw the face, but the departing figure looked like Chu. The thing in his hand was a small peach. It was early for peaches, and as he bit into the fuzz, the sourness made his teeth ring. But he ate it all and sucked the seed for a long time before spitting it to the ground to begin to sing again.

Because they were Feng's men and it was their leader who lay gravely wounded, they were to be allowed to join the vanguard in the attack upon Chuan-chou. Yang called them together for instructions. Wang Lee strained his eyes and ears to focus on the little king. He seemed to be bouncing about on the pile of baggage from which he was speaking, telling which units to enter by which tunnel and which units to rush the gates.

"We have no quarrel with the people of Chuan-chou." He was screaming to be heard. "We seek only to fight in the name of the High God against His enemies the Manchu demons. But these sons of dogs have dared to attack a King of the Heavenly Kingdom. What does the High God command his army to do?"

"Destroy!" a single voice shouted. "Destroy! Destroy! Destroy!" the chant went up. "Destroy!" The word began to invade their bodies, consuming them. There was no more hunger, no more fatigue, only the chant. They rushed into the tunnels, crawled forward on their knees, scurrying like rats through the darkness. They scraped the narrow sides. Pikes, swords, guns — all caught and had to be snatched off and dragged along the dirt. They became dizzy from the lack of air, but they hurried forward in the silent blackness, propelled by the chant that clanged inside their bodies: "Destroy! Destroy! Destroy!"

The first group to enter the city killed the startled sentinels, while the next threw open all four gates of the city. When every sentinel and every homeless beggar lay on the streets of Chuan-chou in his own blood, the gates and doors of houses were battered in. Pleas of mercy could not be heard. The chant drowned them out.

Wang Lee did not bother using his flintlock. It was too slow. A sword did not need reloading and ramming and cocking. He swung it down again and again and again. He could not see faces. It was dark, and most of the turtles were groveling, pressing their foreheads into the dirt, almost begging to be beheaded.

Day came, but the job was not over. Then there was night, and another day. Wang Lee and his men killed an old man and his wife cowering beside their platform bed, left the bodies on the dirt floor, and fell upon the bed in a drugged sleep. When Wang Lee awoke, his head pounding, his men had already thrown out the bodies and had begun cooking millet porridge on the mud stove. They ate without speaking, without looking at one another, threw the empty bowls crashing against the bed, and went out once more into the blinding sunlight. They stumbled on from house to house. In some the stench was already rising, and they knew there was no need to enter.

A fever was raging inside Wang Lee's flesh. He could not hear or see what he was doing. When he saw a woman standing in front of her door, his brain wondered thickly why she was standing there on her tiny pointed feet. Why didn't she kowtow and plead for mercy like the rest? Why was she waiting, her eyes flashing defiance? The unit's new recruit rushed forward, sword raised, but she leapt like a cat off her lily-feet into his chest. Wang Lee saw the butcher knife just before it struck. He drew his own sword. She had time to whisper a single word between her teeth before she died. "Pig." At least that was what he thought he heard.

He stepped over her headless body to push open the door behind her. He did not enter at once but stood outside, staring into the darkness. The woman had meant to stop them. What was she hiding? There was no movement within. He tied on his sword and unslung his gun. His hands were trembling with exhaustion, but somehow he managed the complicated tasks of loading and ramming and cocking. He waited a minute more at the door to let his eyes drink the worst of the darkness. Then he stepped silently over the threshold. He moved quickly into the shadows, so the light from the door would not expose him, and listened. At first there was nothing, then a slight movement on the far side of the bed platform. He could barely make out a form, someone crouching there. He aimed and fired. There was a single sharp almost birdlike cry.

He went cautiously to the bed and leaned over toward the mound. It was very small. A child. Almost a baby. With his left hand he turned the body over. A little girl—not more than two. A streak of black blood ran from her small mouth. The ball had made a neat round hole in her embroidered jacket. There was no breath in her, but he could smell her little mouth, mother's milk still sweet upon her lips.

He turned quickly and left the house. His men stayed. He knew they were looting, but he could not stop them. He leaned against the outside wall and spit. It loosened his throat, and he vomited millet porridge on the cobblestones until it came the taste of bile.

Where could he go? He stumbled through the streets toward the east gate. His feet were black with blood. It had dried even between his toes. If he could get to the river, if he could only wash… He heard the voice of Chu shout for him as he left the gate, but he didn't even turn his face toward the sound.

He started to dive headfirst into the water — clothes, gun, sword and all — but some of the lily-footed women of the Taiping were on the riverbank washing laundry, and one of them called out, "Your gun!" So he continued walking through the thigh-deep water to the far bank. There he climbed out and sat down heavily upon the ground. Then, very carefully, in the manner of an old man clinging to the last of his powers, he began deliberately to remove his pike, his gun, his sword — it was stained, so he wiped it carefully on the grass — his bundle, his turban, his tunic, his sash, his grass sandals. He looked upriver to see if the women were watching. They were gossiping and beating their clothes on the rocks, so he stripped to his loincloth. He folded his trousers carefully and stacked them neatly with his other garments, and then he walked into the water and stooped down. For a while he stayed there, kneeling neck deep, clouding the water with the grime and blood from his body, waiting until the current carried the defilement away. Then he put his face in. The surface of the water was warm from the June sun. He opened his eyes and looked at the shimmering stones — like the pavement of some celestial city. How easy it would be for him never to raise his face. "What a pity… what a pity… what a pity…" Abruptly he brought his face up and lay back. His long hair spread about his face in a black fan. He felt as though he were floating and, for a moment, lifted his feet and sank to the bottom. He could stay here. He could hide forever. "What a pity…" The words were sharp and accusing now, as the complaints of crows picking the rocky earth in an empty field. His feet hit the stones, slipped on their slickness, but he curled his toes and forced himself to his feet. It was not so easy after all.

Coughing and choking, he fetched his filthy clothing from the bank and plunged it into the water. He swirled the garments round and round until he was surrounded by a giant brown cloud. Should he beat them on a rock the way the women were? He knew suddenly he could not. He staggered to the bank and dropped his sopping clothes in a heap upon his gun and sword before he fell down beside them more weary than a graveless ghost.

It was dark when he awoke from his stupor. Someone was kneeling over him, speaking to him, her long hair brushing his cheek. "Little brother, you must come back before you are missed."

He roused himself to an elbow, the effort making his head spin. "I was very tired," he said.

"Yes, that is why Chu sent me. I have the horse."

He could make out the lines of it now, its long neck bent over the river he had polluted. He could hear it lapping the water, shuddering and stomping. It tossed its mane back and bent to drink again.

"It is not right…." he began.

"Here," Mei Lin said, "let me help you." She was pulling his still wet trousers over his legs. "Can you stand?"

"Of course," he said. But he almost fell when he tried.

She held him up with her upper arms and from behind tied the string of his trousers quickly like a mother dressing a small boy who is struggling to run from her. He dropped to the ground. She pulled him by the arm to a sitting position and then began to thread the sleeves of his tunic onto his arms. He helped now as best he could. Life was trickling into his limbs once again. She leaned close to wrap his sash about his waist, and he could feel her breasts against his chest, warm through the wetness of his garment. It was not lewdness, not the lust of an animal that seized him, but a great ache surging through his body. He wanted her to hold him. He wanted to hide himself in her silken warmth.

"There," she said. "Your sandals are already in the bundle. Get your sword and gun. It's wet, but perhaps not ruined."

"Mei Lin…"

"Come along." She was not hearing the plea in his voice. She was all soldier now — no, all mother. He was nothing but a tired and naughty child. She called her horse with a low whistle. When it came she made a sling with her clasped hands beside its belly. "Step here," she ordered. "Your right foot here. Your left goes across its back."

He did not move. He was afraid to touch her skin even with his foot.

"It is late. We must go back."

"You go," he said. "I can walk."

"Are you all right?"

"Yes," he lied.

She looked him hard in the face, ready to argue, but seemed to think better of it, simply sighing and throwing her hair back over her shoulder. "Then go in health, my brother," she said. She mounted and clicked her tongue at the horse. He watched them plunge into the river and head back across the fields toward the tents outside the city gate.

In his own tent, he found his men still awake. They did not speak of his absence or of the death of the recruit, only of the plunder. They had had to contribute all the goods they had looted to the central treasury, but they wanted to brag to him of the riches they had given up — a bit of silver, some silks, rice, millet, salt.... He nodded and tried to praise them a little for resisting temptation to keep anything for themselves.

"You respected the Heavenly Precepts. Good," he said. "Very good." But the commandments so clean and clear upon the printed page swam red before his eyes. "Six: Do not kill...." He heard again the birdlike cry of the baby and her mother's curse. The old people lay crumpled and bleeding beside their bed. "What a pity that men should kill each other." It was Shen's voice coming out of a face with empty sockets for eyes. "Seven: Do not commit adultery or harbor lewdness...." Now the voice was no longer Shen's but hers. He jumped up, hitting his head on the low slung canopy, causing the tent pole to shudder.

"Sergeant?"

They mustn't worry. Wang Lee sat down carefully. "I remembered some business, but it can wait." He led them in evening prayers then, as though this day had been no different from any other.

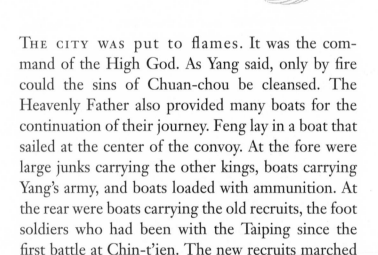

# CHAPTER FOURTEEN
## SOUNDS OF MOURNING

THE CITY WAS put to flames. It was the command of the High God. As Yang said, only by fire could the sins of Chuan-chou be cleansed. The Heavenly Father also provided many boats for the continuation of their journey. Feng lay in a boat that sailed at the center of the convoy. At the fore were large junks carrying the other kings, boats carrying Yang's army, and boats loaded with ammunition. At the rear were boats carrying the old recruits, the foot soldiers who had been with the Taiping since the first battle at Chin-t'ien. The new recruits marched down the banks behind the cavalry.

Wang Lee lay on his back, staring at the blue sky of early summer. The river rocked the boat gently forward on the current. There was no sound except the call of birds from the eastern bank, the buzzing of insects, and the quiet *swish* of clear water along the prow. There were no shouts, no hymns, no chants. It was Nirvana — a dream of perfect peace. He willed his mind to blankness. Chu sighed and leaned toward him to whisper, "Three days of this and my old soul may have time to catch up with my body." Wang Lee simply nodded without opening his eyes or mouth. A fly landed on his cheek, but he did not bother even to shake his head.

He must have fallen asleep, because at first the shouting seemed to be part of a dream; but then there was a jolt. He jumped to his feet. Their small boat had rammed into the one ahead of it. Farther ahead he could see a jumble of boats hard against one another, row on row all the way to the junks that carried the kings.

Word passed quickly deck to deck. The lead junks had somehow become entangled in fishing nets set just below the surface of the water. There was no need to panic. The convoy would move forward as soon as the nets were cut. Meantime… But there was to be no meantime. Before the nets could be cut away, Imperial troops rose up from the grass on the western bank and opened fire.

It was an ambush worthy of Feng, Wang Lee thought grimly. The enemy now used his own strategy against him. Wang Lee's mind moved from a dream of peace to the trance of war. He did not have to decide or will or do. His body performed like a windup toy — fire, load, ram, cock, aim; fire, load, ram, cock, aim; fire again. Every shot must eliminate a demon. When the cavalry arrived, and after them the new recruits, the old recruits were ordered to the eastern shore. They waded across the river and flung themselves on the bank. There they sat or squatted, watching the horror on the other side. For a moment Wang Lee thought he saw horses and the yellow and red of San-niang's women. Where was Mei Lin? His eyes burning with the strain of looking, he thought he saw her. There she was, in the midst of the confusion, no, perhaps there.... It was too far and the battle too intense ever to be sure. *May the High God deliver her.*

Feng had been brought ashore and a tent erected over the spot where he lay. "They say he is dying," Chu said, wiping the sweat and grime from his face with the tail of his tunic. "He spurts fresh blood."

The demons were shooting fire arrows now. Crimson and canary flames transformed the brown grass roofing of the little boats like wild flowers springing up after a drought. Then the explosions began, the noise shattering the senses. Wang Lee covered his ears and closed his eyes to shut out the pain, but it grew louder and more exquisite, piercing deep into the center of his skull. The ground moved beneath him, throwing his body against Chu, who was screaming as he fell. "The gunpowder! The demons hit the gunpowder!"

Where was Mei Lin? He could see nothing on the other side of the burning river. He tried to hold her in his mind, seeing her as immortal — a goddess warrior — her gold and crimson garments swirling about her body, her shaggy little gray horse grown huge, protected all about by guardian spirits, invulnerable to men or demons. But suddenly her swirling garments turned to enveloping flames. He put his hands to his face to shut out the sight.

At last the explosions were spent. They no longer shook the earth but popped and snapped like strings of festival firecrackers. Once more from the western bank, they could hear the noise of combat — rifle reports, clang of metal on metal, and the ghostly cries of those killing and being killed. The rebel gong sounded the unfamiliar order to retreat. And those on the eastern bank watched every break in the smoke and flames for the first sight of escaping brethren. A few came through — a pitiful few. Some of them drowned in the shallow water, too injured or exhausted to make their way around the burning debris. Those who could be seen in time were saved — or at least dragged out to die upon the shore.

But the old recruits could not devote themselves to the dead and dying. The order had been given to re-form the lines. When the Imperial troops followed up their advantage and crossed the river to finish what they had begun, the cost of victory must come high. The rebels waited. They had lost nearly all their gunpowder, so it would be a battle like those of the early days — swords and pikes and hoes and kitchen knives and feet and fists and teeth.

As he waited, Wang Lee groomed his soul for death. He did not point his head toward Paradise but toward the emptiness of this world. She had not returned. None of San-niang's women had come across the river. He did not dare ask for word. His face and voice would betray him. Anyone he asked would surely know that he had committed sin, in his heart; and if he no longer cared for his own life, he would not bring dishonor to her memory.

The June evening was hot and still. But he waited in a kind of coldness. Death was sure to come by morning. And it did come, but not his own. It was Feng who died.

As the news spread, a shrill keen of mourning rose from the camp and could not be hushed. At first Yang tried to remind those who brought the word that mourning for the dead was forbidden — that in the Heavenly Kingdom the passage to Paradise is glorious and must be celebrated. But the Taiping would not be denied this grief. Feng was dead, "Aieeee." Feng, their Southern King, their teacher, their elder brother, was dead. The very heavens wept, putting out the last flames upon the river.

Wang Lee's mourning cry was stuck in his wooden throat. He could not cry out to Heaven. He beat his breast with his fist instead. It is finished. It is all over. The Kingdom is no more. Feng is dead. But Mei Lin will never know. He found a tiny comfort in the thought. She would never have to suffer this loss.

At dawn they remained at their posts, the weeping exhausted. And still the demons had not struck. Wang Lee, who had been ready for death a few hours before, was now concerned with the stiffness of his body. He twisted his right arm and hunched and lowered his shoulder. Why didn't the sons of turtles come and get it over with? Feng would have laughed at them. And where were the Imperial reserves that should have been hidden on the eastern side of the river, ready to rush in and annihilate the crippled Taiping? They hadn't learned from Feng as much as he'd thought.

"They come! They come!" the shout went up, and the gongs were sounded. A faint thunder of cavalry could be heard. At last, the fools.

Then suddenly, confusion. One lookout was screaming something to the next. Finally a name was called back and forth across the rebel lines and echoed throughout the camp. "San-niang! San-niang!" It was not the enemy, but the horsewomen of San-niang galloping in from the north.

The rain had stopped, and now the sun burst out, the yellow of the horsewomen's tunics dazzling the eyes of the waiting rebels. A few young privates broke ranks and ran toward the women. No one called them back. Even the most disciplined veterans were shouting, waving their guns or pikes in the air. Wang Lee stood paralyzed and silent until he saw Mei Lin's face. She was beside San-niang as usual, their horses surrounded by cheering soldiers so that the women could neither move nor dismount. But it was all right. He had seen her and she was safe. The High God had heard his prayer.

It was an hour or more before the crowd began to disperse and she made her way to where he was standing. He could hardly see her for the tears in his eyes. He put his face against the horse's neck to hide his weeping. He could feel her hand on his head.

"There," she said, "there. He would not have us mourn."

She thought he was weeping for Feng. He did not lift his head.

"And yet" — the pressure of her hand was gone and her voice broke now with the words — "how can I keep my soul from grief?" She was fighting for control. "My teacher is dead. I prayed that the High God would let me die in his place. But God did not listen to me. Why didn't He listen to me?"

"I asked that your life be spared," he said quietly, not daring to look at her.

She slid off her mount and stood beside him. "What right do you have to pray such a prayer?" Her voice was low and charged with anger.

"No right," he said.

"And why should the High God listen to you and not to me?"

"I do not know."

"He is dead," she said hoarsely to keep from shouting out. "Feng is dead. Who will teach us now?"

He shook his head. It was almost too heavy to move.

"How could you understand? He was my true father, my true elder brother, my true... I saved his life once, twice — Why was I not allowed to save it a third time?"

He did not try to answer.

"And you dare pray for my miserable life. What is my life to you?"

"You… you are my teacher. And you have saved my life… and…"

"And?"

"I cannot say it."

"Say it," she commanded.

He turned from her and put his right hand on the mane of the horse and stared across its neck at the wreckage on the river. The horse quivered under his hand. "I cannot say it without sinning."

"If it is in your heart, the sin is already there."

He picked at a matted place in the horse's mane. "I pray for your life because it is my heart's treasure."

"Because you are my younger brother."

"No."

"I don't understand you."

He was ashamed and angry and glad all at the same time, and it made his voice gruff. "Why is it so strange that I should desire you? You are more lovely than the Kingdom."

Now he had said it, he looked brazenly into her face and was startled to see something like fear in her eyes.

"No," she said, "no," shaking her head. She swung herself up on the back of the beast, who shuddered as though with pleasure. "No. God forgive you. Go and wash and beg mercy." She clucked to the horse and dug her bare heels into its flanks.

He watched her go, and then he walked to the riverbank. But he could not immerse himself in the water. It was fouled with death.

## CHAPTER FIFTEEN
# HOMECOMING

THE DEMONS did not come that day or the next. Feng was buried with the celebration befitting a ruler of the Heavenly Kingdom of Great Peace. The troops were directed not to mourn. The Heavenly King himself delivered the proclamation.

"Our brother, the Southern King, has ascended into Paradise. He stands even now in the presence of the High God our Heavenly Father and His Elder Son Jesus. The King's body will be buried here in the earth. Do not say: 'How pitiful that the body of Feng lies so far from the graves of his ancestors.' All men are brothers, sons of the High God. All earth becomes for us the place of our ancestors. We are not as the ignorant heathen. We are Children of God who know that the four corners of the earth belong to His Heavenly Kingdom and the death of the flesh is merely the glory of the Spirit entering the Celestial Realm."

The proclamation lasted for more than an hour. Then hymns were sung and prayers recited. When the service was completed, the order was given to break camp. But they were not going to continue toward Changsha, the provincial capital, not in their present state. Instead they would go into the southern corner of Hunan Province, where spies had assured Yang that the Taiping had many friends.

The city of Tao-chou was delivered into rebel hands by a grateful citizenry. There was no need for weapons. The sojourn in that place might have been remembered with pleasure, except for one incident. Someone revealed to the kings that the father of Hsiao, the Western King, had sent for his wife and slept with her in defiance of the law of separation. Hsiao, in righteous anger, summoned his parents before the council of the kings, denounced the old people guilty of lewdness, and ordered them beheaded. He then sent word for his sister to come and witness the execution.

Mei Lin was with San-niang when the king's messenger brought the summons. Indeed, when the messenger had left the house, Mei Lin read the message to her commander, because San-niang, the daughter of a charcoal bearer, had never learned to read.

The words pierced Mei Lin's body like points of cold steel. Her voice faltered.

"What? I don't understand," San-niang said.

"The Western King has condemned his parents

because they have been found guilty and confessed to the sin of…"

"My parents would not sin." She shook her head. "They are old. They have been married thirty years."

Mei Lin did not answer. What harm could it do the Heavenly Kingdom for two old people to find comfort in each other's embrace? Still, the commandment was known. There was no excuse.

"How can he order the death of our parents?" San-niang asked, slowly understanding what was meant. "They gave us everything. They went hungry themselves to put food in our mouths. They went barefoot in winter so that we could have sandals. Even now when their children have been exalted in the Heavenly Kingdom, they have asked for nothing from us."

Quickly Mei Lin touched her fingers to the commander's lips. No one outside the door must hear her grief. It might sound like disloyalty. And if the Western King had no pity for his parents — She shuddered.

"I cannot obey," San-niang whispered. "Help me, little sister. I cannot watch them die." She sent Mei Lin to the market to buy an herb which she boiled into a soup and drank, and within hours tossed on her quilt with a raging fever. Meantime, the parents were brought to the marketplace of Tao-chou to be executed. The Western King, who could hardly read himself, had a scribe read aloud from the proclamations those words concerning true loyalty.

"When it is impossible to obey both one's parents and the High God, one must obey the High God." He caused to be read again all the declarations against lewdness and adultery. And after the sword had fallen twice, he rose from his yellow chair and said in a voice loud enough for the whole assembly to hear, "Parents who violate the Heavenly Precepts are not parents."

Mei Lin stayed beside her commander night and day, wiping her forehead with a wet cloth and soothing her feverish cries in the tones of an old family nurse. But her mind was remembering stories from the old teachings.

"Suppose," a disciple asked the teacher Mencius, "the father of the emperor should murder a man. What should the minister of justice do?"

"Why, the minister would have to arrest the murderer."

"Shouldn't the emperor, out of duty to his father, forbid the arrest?"

"The emperor, of all people, cannot go against the law."

"Then what should the emperor do?"

"The righteous emperor would regard the abandonment of the kingdom like the casting away of a worn-out sandal. He would put his old father on his back and secretly carry him to a place of hiding. There he would live out his life in happiness, forgetting the kingdom."

Feng had told her that story—Feng, who had also taught her one of the earliest declarations of the

Heavenly King: "You should not kill one innocent person or do one unrighteous act, even though it be to acquire an empire." She had not heard this declaration repeated for a long time. But the old man and woman had broken the commandment. Discipline must be maintained — especially now. Suddenly she saw that arrogant boy, that foolish arrogant boy, weeping against her horse. The tears of a friend are more dangerous than the sword of an enemy. She must avoid him at all costs. She must not let him drag them both to destruction.

It was midsummer, but the death of the old parents of the Western King put the Taiping in the grip of such a coldness that even the Heavenly King — as removed as he kept himself from earthly affairs — felt the chill. He declared that the High God had given them a time of rest and rebuilding. The printers were to set work printing the Good News of the Heavenly Kingdom, and then there was a call for volunteers to distribute the flyers throughout the neighboring countryside and win new recruits.

Chu suggested to Wang Lee that the two of them volunteer. The night before they were due to set out, a messenger came from Yang ordering Wang Lee and Chu to come to the house where the king was quartered. The sentry led them through a series of gates and courtyards to a large room off the innermost courtyard. The king was in his yellow robes seated in his yellow chair. In the light of the peanut-oil lamps, his face was yellow as well. His sparse mustache was a straggly shadow on his lip.

But Wang Lee hardly saw his face. As soon as he and Chu crossed the threshold, the guard ordered them to fall upon their hands and knees and bump their foreheads on the stone-paved floor.

"The young sergeant is from Hunan Province." Yang was not asking.

"This miserable person was born in the shadow of Heng Mountain in a village worth no regard." Wang Lee thought it wise to be as polite as he knew how.

The king, however, did not seem to notice. "That is more than halfway to the city of Changsha. You have never been to Changsha."

"This miserable person has never…"

"Money will be provided. You will go by river. You will bring me word before the summer is over. We want to know where the demons are, how many they are, and how well Changsha is defended."

His heart went as cold as the paving under his forehead. A spy.

"We have called the barbers. For the time being you must submit to having your head shaved and the crown hair braided in the manner prescribed by the demons."

The companions were led out of the dim audience room into the torchlit courtyard where the barbers waited, stools in place. They shaved all of Wang Lee's and Chu's heads except for the crown, and then carefully braided the long remaining hair into a queue. Wang Lee's scalp itched and crawled. He felt strangely ashamed of its nakedness.

"Ha! You shell-less turtle!" Chu, seeing his discomfort, poked fun at his head in the raw language of a charcoal bearer.

The insult was better than a tonic. "And what are you? You bottom of a plucked rooster!"

They slapped each other on the back, each asking choice questions about the ancestry of the other's mother. Then, provided with the faded blue garments of peasants, they took off their tunics with the rhinoceros emblems and their bright blue trousers. They were sent back to their own house to make their bundles. Each carried a bowl, chopsticks, and a small sack of rice bound up in his quilt and tied to his back. Chu tied a copper teakettle to his belt, and Wang Lee tied a water gourd to his. They were to carry no weapons. At first Wang Lee added to his bundle the book that Mei Lin had given him, and then, reluctantly, took it out and gave it to his corporal for safekeeping. If he were caught with a Taiping book in his pack, it would cost both of them their lives.

When they were ready, they went as directed to the north gate, which was cracked to let them slide out into the star-filled summer night.

They agreed that when words were needed, Wang Lee would speak for them both. They were in Hunan now, and his speech was that of a Hunanese peasant. It was well known that the Taiping swarmed with charcoal bearers from the mountains of Kwangsi. They pretended to be farmers who had taken their rice and sold it to the Imperial army for a handsome price and then spent nearly all their profit gambling on the trip home. The boatmen, who had no love for the army, treated them royally. How delightful it must be to cheat the turtles and live, even for a short time, a life of ease and pleasure! Why should such men be prudent? It was best to enjoy one month of this miserable existence to the full. In the presence of such wise and happy fellows, the boatmen grew expansive. They pulled out their pipes and put in a pinch of tobacco or opium, leaned back against the stern, and talked long into the night. There was always a bit of breeze on the river at night and plenty of food. It was a fat and pleasant time. Even Wang Lee's dreams grew dim — the faces of Mei Lin and Shen appearing less and less to trouble him as the days went by.

Then suddenly one morning he looked up from the deck and recognized Heng Mountain towering up from the plain. Beyond the cattails and rushes were paddies ready for the second rice planting, and across the paddy water he could see cabbage and turnips and onions springing from the red soil of his birth. His heart leaned toward that red earth as an infant toward its mother's outspread arms. He wanted to go home. He wanted to see the farm of his ancestors. He wanted to smell his father's land and hear his father's voice. He even wanted to see his mother's lily-feet and pinched little face. It was only a few li to the east. They could go and return in half a day.

Chu was not pleased with the idea. They were

moving along well. At this rate they could be in Changsha in a few days. "You know the recent declaration of the King, little brother, that in obedience to the Kingdom, we cannot give thought even to our parents."

"Yes," said Wang Lee, glimpsing about to make sure the boatmen were out of earshot.

Chu sighed. "It is easy for me. I have no family except the Heavenly Army." He smiled a yellow snaggle-toothed smile. "Go in health, little brother," he whispered. "I will wait just here, upon the bank."

Wang Lee left his bundle and gourd in Chu's care and set off across the fields. They were a patchwork of varying green, still rich with the smell of night soil. His father would be having a good harvest this year. He would want Wang Lee to stay. He would need the boy's help. How could he explain to his father that he must return immediately? The old man would not understand any duty greater than that to the land of one's ancestors. But it could not be helped. When the triumph was complete, when the Heavenly King reigned from Nanking, he would return and be a more dutiful son than even Confucius could have imagined. And the land would be safe, then. No more soldiers or bandits. The dikes would be rebuilt against the threat of floods. All people and nature would live in the harmony of Great Peace. Perhaps his father could not understand this now, but in time Wang Lee would show him.

He broke into a trot, the unfamiliar pigtail

flapping on his neck. But the landscape was no longer foreign. It was the intimate little country of his boyhood. There he had walked the old water buffalo. He had chased a runaway pig up that treeless mound. He had taken that path to market. And there, up on that hillside, were the graves of his ancestors. And here, just here… but he stopped. His breath came in painful gasps, tearing at his throat. This was his father's land. Why was it overgrown with vines and weeds? Where was his father? His mother? The house stood as always on its patch of beaten red earth with the persimmon tree by its door. He ran to it, lifting his heavy feet and forcing himself along the path, not wanting to know and yet having to find out. He burst through the small wooden door.

There was a sound of scuffling and confusion in the darkness of the room, and then an old, nearly forgotten voice said, "Well — I'll be born of a dog's mother. It's the pigboy come home."

# CHAPTER SIXTEEN
## SPY IN CHANGSHA

HE TURNED TO RUN, but a gun barrel was jammed against his backbone. Perhaps he should run anyway and let the sons of turtles blow him into the Celestial Kingdom, but some base desire made him choose life. He stood in the doorway, his chest still heaving from his race home.

"Take him into the sunlight and let's have a look at him," Red Eye said. The rifle dug into his back, and he stumbled forward over the threshold onto the beaten earth of the courtyard. "Now. Turn around slowly. Any tricks and you're crow feed."

He turned to face them. Red Eye and Pinch Face were as ugly and dirty as ever. Red Eye's diseased eye was, if anything, redder and more repugnant. Short Neck was not with them, but there was a new companion, squat and dark as a Cantonese pirate. Short Neck must have fallen asleep at the wrong time. Another difference was their clothing. The bandits had exchanged their rags for the baggy tunics and trousers of the Imperial army.

Red Eye was looking him over as well. "Let's see, how long has it been now?" He squinted his one good eye. "One year? Two years? Nearly two since I sold you to that scoundrel in Kweilin. What a thief he was!" Then he began to laugh. Pinch Face and the dark one, who was holding the rifle, looked at him in puzzlement. Red Eye was laughing so hard he could scarcely speak. Finally, he squawked out, "There's justice under Heaven. I was cheated, so Heaven sent my property flying into my arms once more." He slapped his palms together and looked heavenward in a mock pose of gratitude. "Thank you, gracious gods. I will not be cheated a second time. Now," he barked, "hobble him so he can't run. Get your things, and we'll be on our way. In Changsha a boy like this will fetch a pretty price."

They were headed more north than west. Wang Lee realized at once that they would come to the river well beyond the place where Chu was waiting. How strangely fate had treated him. It was his punishment. He had not kept his mind single. He had longed to see his parents when his only thought should have been his duty. It was a sin that could not be forgiven.

Pinch Face had taken his dirty kerchief and tied one end securely to each of Wang Lee's ankles, leaving him able to walk only in short, choppy steps. The boy had to think about his feet or he would forget and try to take a normal stride and trip himself in the attempt. His hands were tied behind his back, so he could not wipe away the sweat that poured down his shaven head from the crown, or brush away the flies that rose from the manure in the fields to settle on his nose or lips. He jerked his head and wriggled his nose. It made him think of Mei Lin's little gray horse.

The bandits did not speak of his parents. He strained his ears in case they let something drop, but he did not ask. Red Eye would probably tell him some monstrous lie so that they could laugh when he believed it, or he might tell an equally monstrous truth. Wang Lee did not want either. He chose to imagine his parents leaving soon after he had left two years ago, going south where there was promise of food and work. That was what peasants did in times of famine. Someday soon they would come home again. He wondered if the seed rice was still behind the brick.

The bandits had searched him before they left the farmyard and had taken the money he had hidden in his sash, so that when they got to the river, they hailed a boat bound for Changsha and ensconced themselves in a corner of the deck. They explained to the boatman that Wang Lee was a deserter whom they had bravely recaptured. The boatman flashed the boy a look of pity. Perhaps, thought Wang Lee, the man would help him escape. But when he saw how cowed the man was by the presence of soldiers on his boat, he gave up hope of help.

It was a hot July day on the river. The bandits, stripped to their loincloths, reclined against baskets of rice and vegetables, acting like wealthy men on a pleasure cruise. Any moment they would begin spouting poetry. Wang Lee's legs were stretched out in front of him, still tied together. His hands were behind him, bent up from the splintery deck. He tried to concentrate by singing hymns inside his head and, when that didn't work, reviewing characters he had memorized, drawing the strokes mentally. Before the day was out, he had given himself over to inventing new curses against Red Eye and his ant-headed companions.

"Perhaps we should keep the pigboy," Red Eye was saying.

"What do you mean, keep him?" Pinch Face sputtered over his tea. "He's bigger and stronger than ever. We could get at least a hundred taels of silver for him now."

"But the boy is like a lucky piece. When we have him, life is nothing but good fortune. Look at us now. The boatman is feeding us for free. Giving us tea whenever we ask. He's promised us wine at the next town.... Remember what happened last time we sold him? Two days and we were back in the army. Three, and Short Neck was deader than your grandmother."

"A hundred taels of silver is luck enough," said Pinch Face. "We could buy our way out of this turtle-dirt army with money like that."

The bandits were careful. They drank, but never to the point of drunkenness. When night came, one was always awake and on guard. They untied Wang Lee only to allow him to eat and relieve himself, and the gun was always loaded and cocked. By the third day, the boy was near despair. He could see no way to escape. And then, downriver on the east bank, rose the walls of Changsha. He was being taken by Imperial soldiers into the city. The bandits were helping him do his duty. That was why Heaven had delivered him into their hands. After he got the information for which he had been sent, Heaven would help him get away. In the meantime, he was still a spy for the Taiping. He only wished he could get word to Chu, whom he pictured waiting faithfully on the riverbank near Heng Mountain.

The great west gate of the city was open, and in the shadow of the wall, merchants had set up their stalls. The place crawled with life like a manure hole in summer. There were itinerant bankers with strings of copper cash and barbers and dentists with their stools and tools upon their backs, ready to go to work at the flash of a coin. There were fishmongers, noodle and dumpling sellers, umbrella menders, sandal makers, and candy men with foot-long sticks of sugar sweets. There were strolling bands of soldiers, beggars crying out for pity and a copper, street players and musicians performing for gawking farmers. Street urchins had caught cicadas in the banyan trees and tied strings about their bellies so that the poor tormented little creatures would sing and sing. The noisy ones sold quickly.

The bandits had untied Wang Lee so as not to

draw attention to themselves, but they kept shoulder-close to him, and their knives were in their sleeves. Unlike the Taiping, the Imperial army had no special quarters. Soldiers stayed wherever they could buy or bully lodging. The bandits took Wang Lee to an inn not far from the west gate. Red Eye directed the other two to stay with him, while he went to a merchant he knew to try to arrange a sale. "As much as I hate to let my little pig go…"

But he was back in less than an hour. Selling a slave was not going to be as easy as he thought. The long-haired rebels had crossed the border into Hunan. They would be heading for Changsha before long. Some of the wealthy had already fled northward. Those who remained were in no mood to spend money that would be needed for bribes, transportation, even necessities, in case of siege.

"You and your lucky little pigboy," grumbled their Cantonese companion. "We'd be better off if he were a pig. Then at least we could eat him."

"Or a donkey. Then we could rent him out," said Pinch Face.

"Can wisdom be found in the mouth of a turtle? That's it! We rented him out before. Why not again? Not on the river — he might swim away. But look at him — arms like gateposts, legs like banyan trunks. What a clever dog you are!" With that Red Eye jumped to his feet and left the inn courtyard again. This time when he returned, he was smiling and rubbing his grubby palms together. The pigboy was hired out as a sedan chair carrier.

Pinch Face spit in the dirt. "We won't get wealthy off his wages carrying a chair. Those turtles hardly make enough to wet their own mouths."

"True enough. Think of it as a pickle crock."

"A what?"

"A pickle crock. A place to keep a morsel while it ripens. When the time is right, we take off the lid...." He made a great lip-smacking sound. "Meantime, our tasty little turnip is preserved without our having to feed him."

The Cantonese bandit let out a great guffaw. Even Pinch Face half smiled. But Wang Lee, sitting silently beside him, kept his own face smooth as a melon. He could already smell escape.

Carrying a sedan chair was every bit as difficult as towing a riverboat, perhaps more so, since the bearers had to work as a team. Wang Lee was one of four men assigned to a single large chair. Two were between the poles in front of the chair and two behind. The others cursed him and kicked him if he stumbled or broke rhythm, but he was larger and stronger than he had been two years before, and so he was soon able to carry his share without causing strain for his companions. They were ignorant country men whose only pleasure was an occasional whiff of opium. Wang Lee's heart went out to them. They were like Chu, except that they had no vision of a Heavenly Kingdom. For the first time since his baptism, he felt a desire to preach, but he did not dare. If he so much as hinted that he had ever been near the long-haired rebels, his head would soon leave his shoulders. This was the time for looking and listening, not for speaking.

It was late August when he heard the news that filled him with joyful confusion. The Taiping were on the move. They had left Tao-chou and fought their way northward to the walled city of Chen-chou.

Old Mao, the oldest of the carriers, was retelling the story. "The long-hairs have women warriors — not mortal women, some say, but ghosts. The ghost women rode to Chen-chou on their spirit horses and put a spell on every living creature from cockroach to long-robed official. While the city was bewitched, the barefoot ghosts climbed over the walls in the blackest hour of the night. They killed the officials and the soldiers — split their throats with silver knives and drank their blood."

A shudder went through the hut that served as the carriers' lodging place. "Sometimes they kill everyone," a voice said.

"No," said Mao, "only the rich and evil. They are merciful to the poor."

"I heard they are like the long-nose devils. They boil little children and devour their eyeballs."

A gasp.

"Turtle dirt," said Mao. "The innocent have nothing to fear from the long-hairs — only the Manchu and their running dogs."

"Shhhhh."

Mao laughed. "Let the turtle soldiers hear me. My old tough neck would notch their swords."

"When will the long-haired devils get here?" The question was whispered.

"Well, if those rebel dogs are as clever as they claim," answered Mao in his normal shrill voice, "they'll get here fast before the reinforcements arrive from Nanking. But the long-hairs, for all their big talk, waste time burning down temples and preaching nonsense." He shrugged. "Who can guess?"

Reinforcements were on the way. Wang Lee had to escape from the city at once. He had to get the word to Yang. If the Taiping hurried, they could take Changsha before the additional troops arrived. But how was he to leave? He was never alone. All day he trotted about the city under the poles of a sedan chair with three other carriers. He might as well be an ox in harness. At night the ten carriers slept on a common platform bed. One could not get up to relieve himself without two or three others jumping up to join him. The wall surrounding the grounds was not high, half again his own height, but even if he could scale it during the night undetected by the other carriers or the gatekeeper — even if he could make his way through the city streets to the wall — what was he to do then? The city gates were bolted from sundown to sunup. The ramps that led to the top of the wall were well guarded. If he should somehow get past the sentries, he could not fly to safety from a wall that was at least the height of eight men. It seemed hopeless. And then he remembered the tactic that Mei Lin and Chu had used at Chin-t'ien. It was worth a try.

He waited until everyone had finished his nightly bowl of gruel and was sipping the hot water that served as the poor man's tea.

"I wonder…"

"Yes? Listen to that! The little pig has so many brains they argue among themselves."

He pretended not to hear. "I wonder…" he began again.

"Heaven have mercy. Wisdom spills from his head like a Taoist waterfall."

"Shut up." It was Old Mao speaking, so the heckler obeyed. "What troubles your head, little Pigboy?"

"No," he said, "it is too foolish."

"What is too foolish?" Someone else was interested now.

"Those bandits who brought me here from my father's land. Their heads were not shaved when I first saw them. I thought only that they had been too far from a barber, but now…"

"Long-hairs." Someone breathed the feared name.

"No, impossible," Wang Lee said. "They were only bandits. Still…"

"Still what?"

"If I knew what it was they had buried…"

"Buried?"

"After the tail-less turtles drove my parents away, they made me dig a hole. But they would not let me see what they put in it."

"The long-hairs have the treasures of the south."

He could almost feel their greed as it gathered to a wave across the darkening courtyard. He did not have to say another word. It was all arranged for him. Tomorrow he and Old Mao, the only carrier any of the others could trust, would pretend to have a fare outside the city. They would go out the gate — but not the same gate by which the pigboy had entered the city. No point in taking chances with their luck. A great discussion followed as to whether the two of them should leave the chair with someone outside the gate or carry it with them for treasure bearing. It was settled when Old Mao roared, "I'll do as I see fit!" The other carriers could somehow cover for them during the time it took to make their way to Wang Lee's father's land and dig up whatever was buried there. It was a good plan. Wang Lee's only pang came with the thought that somewhere along the way he must rid himself of Old Mao. He wished the old man reminded him less of Chu.

The next morning Wang Lee and Old Mao took the lightest chair, fit only for a small woman. They even carried a few fares. But as the sun moved high in the southern sky, they turned their backs on it, and their ears against cries for their services, and they made their way at a good trot toward the north gate of Changsha. The weather was so sultry that the sweat on Wang Lee's body did not evaporate. His tunic and trousers and headcloth were as wet as if he had walked fully clothed into the river. The smells of the crowded city choked his nostrils. Everything seemed to be moldering or rotting or putrefying. Tempers were no better. Old Mao, who ran in the front, shrieked to clear the narrow street. But people simply shrieked back at him and either failed to move or moved so slowly that the carriers were forced to stop in the midst of the smells and dirt and heat and noise.... What was the noise? Gongs and shouts.

"Hurry!" screamed Old Mao. "Those sons of turtles are closing the gate."

## CHAPTER SEVENTEEN
# DAYS OF TESTING

AFTER THE GREAT VICTORY at Chen-chou, San-niang was summoned by the kings to receive a reward for the bravery of her women during the battle for the city.

"I cannot go," she said to Mei Lin. "I cannot look on the face of that one I used to call brother." In her agitation she was walking the dirt floor of the small house where they were quartered. In less than ten steps, she had crossed to the opposite wall. Each time she paced, Mei Lin had to step aside, until finally the colonel gave up on protocol and climbed up on the bed platform to get out of the way of her restless commander. San-niang didn't take any notice. "It is time for my fever to recur," she was saying. "You can go for me to receive the honors. You deserve them more than I anyway."

Mei Lin murmured objections to this, but again San-niang ignored her. "Hsuan-chiao should go, too. She likes to think of herself as the Commander of All the Women. Yes, she should go. She is that one's wife and the blood sister of the Heavenly King. They will rejoice to honor her rather than me. And" — looking down at her once lovely riding clothes that were now stained and torn — "her garments have not been soiled in combat. She will be more pleasant to look upon."

So it was that Mei Lin accompanied Hsuan-chiao into the presence of the kings. In the largest room of the largest house in the city of Chen-chou, Hung, the Heavenly King, sat in his great yellow chair with Yang, the Eastern King, seated at his right hand, and Hsiao, the Western King, seated at his left. Wei, the wealthy farmer of Chin-t'ien, now the Northern King, sat to the left of Hsiao; but at Yang's right, there was an empty yellow chair. The death of Feng broke freshly against Mei Lin's heart like a flood against a weakened dike. She was grateful that the order to kowtow was given, so she could kneel with her face hidden by the stone pavement. It would not do for the kings to see her tears.

A lengthy declaration was read, praising the High God for the great victory, thanking Heaven that through suffering and loss the Taiping had grown stronger, better able to conquer the demon Manchu. Those on their knees and faces were to obey the commandments, keep their hearts devoted to their duty; and when they came into Nanking, their rewards would be beyond counting.

When they were finally commanded to stand,

Mei Lin did so, her face flushed from having stayed so long forehead to the floor. She did not look up, the kings must not think her immodest, but she could feel their powerful eyes upon her and flushed even more darkly. She was not accustomed to the gaze of ordinary men, much less that of kings.

An attendant hung something about her neck. Head still bowed, she saw a white jade pendant with writing carved into it, strung on a silk cord. Later walking home, she read the tiny characters. They were an account of the scaling of the wall by San-niang's women, ending with the phrase "God be adored."

San-niang was delirious with fever, but Mei Lin put the cool stone against her burning cheek and told her the words that were carved into its face. She prayed then that San-niang would recover quickly, not only from the self-induced illness but from that darker sickness that threatened her very soul.

By late afternoon the fever burned so hotly that to touch San-niang's skin was like putting a finger on a boiling kettle. Mei Lin was alarmed. It was not enough simply to wipe the commander's face. She rolled back the quilt and slipped San-niang's outer garments off her legs and shoulders to bathe her limbs. It was then that Mei Lin saw the strange ornament lying between San-niang's breasts. On a string of tiny wooden beads such as a Buddhist monk or nun might wear was the carved figure of a man dressed only in a loincloth, writhing as though in pain. She bent closer. Yes. The figure of the Elder

Brother in death. Someone had made an idol of it, in defiance of the Heavenly Precepts. The long-nose Jesus people, perhaps. Quickly she pulled San-niang's tunic together. The penalty for idolatry was death. No one must see this idol.

San-niang stopped tossing and turned toward Mei Lin. Her eyes shone as hard and black as sticks of new ink. One hot hand went up to her breasts to cover the figure, as though she feared Mei Lin might try to snatch it from her. "God descended to earth," she said, but Mei Lin could not tell if the commander was speaking in her own mind or that of the demon fever that possessed her.

She was better, but not yet able to leave the bed, when Hsuan-chiao sent word to the house that she wished to see Mei Lin. Did she suspect San-niang's illness? Mei Lin did not dare wait even for the new garments that had been ordered from the lily-footed women. She washed as best she could with what water was in the house and hurried unattended to the large house where the Commander of All the Women made her headquarters. Above the ordinary smells of the street, she could make out the distinct odor of burning wood. It was not the charcoal of cooking fires, but more the smell of a house in flames. She looked up into the thin strip of sky visible from the narrow street and saw smoke. "What is it?" she asked a water peddler who was standing at a gate waiting to be let in. "What's on fire?"

The man glanced at the sky and then at her riding clothes and bowed his head in respect. "This miserable person has no knowledge," he said. He meant of course that he did not wish to tell her what the smoke meant.

It was the sharp-faced woman guard at the commander's gate who told her. The kings had ordered the burning of the great temple of Confucius in Chen-chou. "False learning must be destroyed," the young woman said.

"Yes," said Mei Lin, her face smooth but her heart furrowed. All those books going up in black smoke. The treasures of a thousand years. If only Feng were here. She saw briefly the face of the boy when she had given him his first book. Was he among the soldiers setting torch to the temple?

The Commander of All the Women was clothed in politeness. She hardly allowed Mei Lin to kowtow before she was urging her to a stool. It made Mei Lin wary. She answered every comment about the weather with a murmur of humble agreement. At length the older woman found her way to the subject of San-niang's health. "I am grieved to hear that my husband's younger sister is still ill."

"It is a troubling thing." Mei Lin felt as though she were crossing a rope bridge.

"Can no physician help her?"

"The physicians cannot determine the cause of the fever." The bridge swung out.

Hsuan-chiao made a gesture of impatience as though dismissing the wisdom of doctors like lint from a garment. "What does the colonel think?"

"This miserable person is not qualified to…"

"Nonsense. You are with the deputy commander night and day. What is your opinion of her health?"

"The fever has broken, but the deputy commander remains weak."

"How soon will she be able to ride?"

Ride! Mei Lin struggled to hide her astonishment. Was the army ready to move already? When had the spies returned? She lifted a composed face. "If God is willing, the commander's younger sister will be able to ride in a few weeks."

In the silence that followed, Mei Lin dared to watch the commander. The woman was struggling with some idea, but at length she sighed and said in a sharper tone than before, "It can't be helped. It is the will of Heaven."

Perhaps if Mei Lin waited, Hsuan-chiao would explain herself. At last the Commander of All the Women spoke. "The Western King, whom I am honored to call my husband, is leading a force to Changsha tomorrow. A spy has returned to say that the city is not well fortified at this time. A small select striking force might, with the aid of Heaven, capture the city. He had hoped that the women would be included in that effort." She leaned forward from her chair. "Think of it — the Western King supported in this glorious attack by his wife and sister. The demons would tremble at the sight. Well" — she leaned back with a deeper sigh than before — "it can't be helped." She waved Mei Lin out of the room. She did not send her regards to her sister-in-law. She did not even remember to say "God be adored."

Hsiao and his troops left the city before daybreak. As soon as the news reached their house, San-niang began visibly to improve. She sent no word to the Commander of All the Women. No one but Mei Lin was to know she was better.

For the next few days, San-niang and Mei Lin kept to themselves in the cool of their house. The heat outside was almost unbearable. Only one strange incident disturbed their peace. A messenger from the Heavenly King came to inquire after the health of the deputy commander of the women. Mei Lin met him in the small courtyard and assured him that San-niang was slowly growing stronger. They exchanged bows and salutes of "God be adored," and the King's messenger left. But after she closed the gate, Mei Lin spied something he must have dropped. She went over and picked it up.

Brushed on the bamboo paper were two lines of poetry. Mei Lin did not know the Classics well. She had had just one brief year of study with Feng, so she did not know what poem the lines might have come from or what their meaning was. She did, with a start, recognize the calligraphy. Only one man in the Taiping wrote like that:

*Did you not know that people hide their love,*
*Like the flower that seems too precious to be picked?*

Quickly she stuffed the paper into the folds of her

sash, her face burning with dread. What could it mean? In this time when every heart must be set on the Kingdom, the writing and copying of love poems was unthinkable. It was impossible, yet she knew she was not mistaken. She had seen the same calligraphy on a host of declarations. But how could it be? How could she have in her sash a love poem written in the Heavenly King's own hand? San-niang must never know.

San-niang and Mei Lin were exercising their horses outside the city gate and so were among the first to hear the news that Hsiao had been gravely wounded before the walls of Changsha. They turned their horses over to grooms and hurried back into the city. A messenger was waiting. The wife of the Heavenly King and the wife of the Western King were already counseling together. San-niang was to come at once. Mei Lin went with the deputy commander as far as the door of the room where the two wives were meeting. There she was invited by a lily-footed woman to another room off the same courtyard, offered a seat, and given a cup of tea.

Mei Lin watched as the woman serving her hobbled about on tiny feet. She seldom had anything to do with small-footed women anymore. At one time the Heavenly King had commanded all the lily-footed females to unbind their feet. But it was too late for most. The Hakka king did not realize that years of binding turned feet into little pointed hoofs that would never grow straight again. Without their bindings, the afflicted women could not walk at all. They begged to have their feet rebound. The order was rescinded. The lily-feet were bound up once more. But in the New Age, the Heavenly Kingdom would carry out the Divine intention, and no female child would ever suffer such pain and indignity again. Mei Lin thanked the woman for the tea. Then walking lightly and proudly, feeling the cool stones of the courtyard under her strong bare feet, she went to wait for San-niang.

The horsewomen were to lead the main body of the advance against Changsha — with one change. They were to ride under the banner of Hsuan-chiao, the Commander of All the Women. Mei Lin looked at San-niang, but the deputy commander simply shrugged. If Hsuan-chiao chose to ride at the head of the company going to rescue her wounded husband, how could her deputy object?

They rode out of the city long before dawn. The commanders were uneasy. The departure, made in such haste, did not give them time to collect supplies needed for a long march, but Yang reassured them. They could procure what they needed along the way. The country people were sympathetic and generous to the Taiping cause.

Even though it was October, the heat was still that of summer. They kept well east of the Shiang River, reasoning that the Imperial army would take the water route to the city. Yang did not wish to waste his troops on a major battle before they reached Changsha.

On the day that the peak of Heng Mountain could be seen far to the west, Chu appeared, handed Mei Lin a kerchief-wrapped parcel, and said simply, "Near this place," before hurrying away. She unwrapped the bundle and found inside a book, the same book she had given the boy. So he was dead. Chu wanted her to know.

She ought to rejoice. The one who had asked to be called Pigboy had given his life for the Heavenly Kingdom. Perhaps in Hsiao's troop or perhaps as a spy. At any rate, he had risen to his glory. He had died without disgracing her either with his arrogance or his appetites. She was grateful. Grateful and relieved. Even now the boy was with Feng, feasting in the presence of the Heavenly Father. But when she tried to picture the scene, her body turned cold and heavy like a great flat stone in the midst of the river.

It occurred to her later that the boy had died near the place where he was born, She was secretly glad. He had had a strong feeling for the land of his ancestors. Feng had understood the human longing for one's native piece of earth. He had quoted for her from an old poem the lines:

> *The migrant bird longs for the old wood:*
> *The fish in the tank thinks of its native pool.*

and then laughed at himself for being sentimental. But she understood, too. Even though she had been only a slave, a woman slave at that, she understood the longing. When Nanking was taken, she would be allowed to own property, and that land would go down to her children's children.

She would be remembered by her descendants as "a leopard colonel in the Heavenly Army who won this land for us by her valor." But the boy would have no descendants to remember him....

Not far from the southern wall of Changsha, on the high hill overlooking the city, the Taiping had made their camp. To the west lay the broad river, in the middle of which Orange Island floated like a narrow needle nearly as long as the west wall of the city. From each notch of the crenelated walls, the blind eye of a cannon stared out at the rebel troops. Changsha's reinforcements had already arrived. In his tent in the center of the camp on Miao-kao Hill, Hsiao lay dying.

Yang gathered the soldiers and whipped them into a fury with his preaching. The miners were sent to tunnel under the walls, and did so with great determination. But somehow, as fast as the hole was opened, it was discovered by the demons and stopped up. Volunteers rushed the gates with explosives, but were shot down before they could do any damage. The women galloped out again and again until their horses mouths' foamed, but the metal eyes of the cannons did not fear ghosts.

They had attacked without sufficient preparation, thinking the foe would be weak and soon conquered. But now the supplies of salt and cooking oil were dwindling fast, the gunpowder was almost gone, and the Western King was dead.

When San-niang heard the news of her brother's death, she murmured only, "It is the will of Heaven." Hsuan-chiao, on the other hand, exchanged the yellow and crimson of the women's army for the white garments of widowhood, and retired as the Commander of All the Women. No one reprimanded her for mourning; indeed, the title of her office was left vacant out of respect, as was the title of Western King. And the High God descended to earth and gave the Heavenly King a great jade seal as a symbol of His promise that the days of withdrawal and defeat were nearly past. The Taiping had endured the time of testing. Nanking would soon be theirs.

## CHAPTER EIGHTEEN
# Kitchen Maid in the House of Sung

WANG LEE and Old Mao pushed and kicked their way through the narrow streets, trying desperately to reach the north gate before it closed. The last stroke of the gong had hardly ceased to tremble when they arrived. But the huge ironbound gate was already shut, and the padlocks were in place.

Mao dropped the front poles of the sedan chair so quickly that the back poles bounced painfully on Wang Lee's shoulders. The boy put down his end and went around to where Mao was questioning the ancestry of the gatemen. "Who are your mothers, you sons of sows? It's still the middle of the afternoon. What do you mean closing the gate without a hundred warning strokes? Some people have business outside. Not like you sons of turtles who lie about all day puffing your opium pipes!"

"If the mindless son of a dog pants to have his tail removed by the sword of a long-haired rebel, maybe we should unlock the gate and throw him out!" one of the gatemen screamed, and all the others agreed with appropriate curses. There was nothing to do but go back to the chair stand and wait for the gate to open. But the north gate opened only to allow reinforcements to enter Changsha. Otherwise, all four gates remained padlocked and well guarded against the forces of the Taiping laying siege to the city.

One night at sunset, Wang Lee and Mao had climbed the ramp to the south wall to see the camp of the Taiping on Miao-kao Hill, with its brightly colored tents gleaming in the glow of the sun's last rays. Campfires began to appear. Wang Lee heard — or did he only imagine it? — the hymns of evening prayer. That was before the pounding of the Imperial cannonry blotted out any sound from outside the city. Soon no civilians were allowed on the wall. He learned in the street that a rebel king had been wounded, perhaps killed. He learned, too, that the main body of the Taiping had arrived and that the ghost women were leading the attack. But he could only hear the pounding, or see sometimes a flaming arrow fly across the tiny patch of sky visible above the streets or the courtyard. Then the clanging gong of the fire wagon. The rebels still had no cannons. Surely the miners would dig their way into the city. But no. There were instead many jokes about the stopping up of "rat holes."

The longer the siege continued, the worse business became. Finally the owner of the chair stand decided to close and thus release himself from the obligation to feed the carriers. A disgruntled Red Eye appeared to collect Wang Lee.

"I ought to run you through with my knife and be done with it," the bandit grumbled. "How could I have ever been fool enough to think a son of a pig's mother like you could bring me good luck? Nobody's going to pay a copper cash for you, and, if I don't watch it, you'll be stolen for the turtle-dirt army. I'd be better off if you were a nothing girl." He walked on glumly for a few steps, and then suddenly grabbed Wang Lee by the chin and jerked him around. Red Eye's face was only a few inches from the boy's, his breath sour with old garlic and foul with decaying teeth, his diseased eye runny. His one good eye was studying Wang Lee as though he were a piece of meat of questionable age and pedigree. At last he shoved the boy's chin away and yanked his pigtail as though he were ringing a bell. "Haiii-ya!" Keeping a firm grip on the queue, he dragged the boy through the streets and to the inn where he was staying, as fast as he could make him go.

He left Wang Lee in the care of Pinch Face and the Cantonese and rushed out on another of his mysterious errands. He came back with a large bundle, which he did not untie, and a barber, whom he set immediately to work. The barber reshaved Wang Lee's head — all but the crown from which the queue hung, according to Manchu law. "Now do his face," Red Eye commanded.

"It's a waste of money," Pinch Face complained. "He's only a boy. Less bristles than a suckling pig."

"This is a special occasion," Red Eye explained to the barber. "Sharpen your blade. His old mother likes to see him with a face as smooth as a baby's bottom."

The barber cackled and sharpened the blade on his whetstone.

"You'd think we had strings of cash hanging from our ears," Pinch Nose muttered. Red Eye only smirked.

When the barber had been paid (overpaid to hear Pinch Face tell it) and sent on his way, Red Eye opened his bundle. From it he pulled out a new blue cotton suit and then a large black mass of what looked like hair. He plopped the hair down on Wang Lee's head. "Pity me," he cried, beating his breast. "I'm a poor old farmer who must sell his only daughter lest his sons starve."

"You'll never get away with such a fool trick," said Pinch Face, but the Cantonese was laughing, walking about the boy and studying him from every angle.

"There," said the Cantonese, adjusting the wig. "Not bad. Not beautiful, mind you. No one could call this pig beautiful. But an honest country face. Big strong feet. She could probably carry a water buffalo to market on her back."

"No, no. This one's too good for a farmer's slave," said Red Eye. "I'm taking her to the tallest gate in the city — to the house of the wealthiest official." He was rubbing his palms together as he always did when he smelled money. He turned on Wang Lee, suddenly stern. "If you're careful, no one will suspect. If you're not, I'll kill you and those turtles who hatched you." Then he took something else from the bundle. Wang Lee jerked back instinctively as the sharp razor flashed in the bandit's hand, but Red Eye simply took off the wig and shaved the rest of Wang Lee's head. Then he plopped the wig back down on the boy's tingling head. "Your hair fell out when you had the fever, in case anyone spies this melon head. That's why you have to wear a wig." He handed Wang Lee the clothes. The jacket was a woman's, with a high collar and knotted cloth buttons beginning at the neck and going across the top of the chest and down the left side. It was snug in the shoulders and short in the sleeves—like a cage compared to his loose tunic, which had no buttons at all. The trousers did not reach his ankles and cut across the crotch. But he did not complain, for Red Eye was waving the razor within inches of his throat. "Remember, my little piglet, if you are found out before I leave this city..." And he drew the razor sideways.

Red Eye sold Wang Lee to the honorable House of Sung to be a kitchen maid. The boy went into the women's quarters carrying a kerchief with his quilt and a razor. He felt not so much frightened as silly. All the women giggled at the sight of him. He must seem very stupid and ugly to them. The tallest person in sight, he hunched his shoulders and nodded when spoken to. Perhaps they would think him humble, for he was sure that if he opened his mouth, his voice would betray him.

When he was presented to the Number One Wife, he kept his forehead on the stone floor and prayed his wig would not fall off while she lectured him. Her husband was a graduate of the Hanlin Academy and thus one of the most respected scholars in the empire. *Blah, blah, blah.* She was the eldest daughter of a wealthy merchant and the mother of three healthy sons. *Blah, blah, blah.* The official had two other wives and a concubine for a total of seven sons. *Blah, blah, blah.* On and on she bragged, so that if Wang Lee had been willing to speak, he might have felt compelled to remind the mistress that such boasting would tempt Heaven to strike the family down — if Heaven itself could outlive the boredom. As it was, of course, he simply bumped his head to the pavement when it seemed appropriate. It was a stupid, cheap wig — a fringe of stiff bangs at the front that pushed up when he kowtowed, and two little skinny pigtails jiggling at the back with pink string binding the ends. Wang Lee had to fight the impulse to put his hand on the top of his head to make sure the wig was secure. It felt as though any moment it might spring from his head and plop at the feet of the mistress like a ball from a long-nose cannon.

"Little Pearl! You!"

It was his name. Another of Red Eye's jokes. How was he to remember to answer to such a name? He mumbled something into the gray stone.

"You may go. The cook will show you where to put your things."

Again he mumbled something and edged his way backward on his hands and knees. As soon as he was out of her sight, he clamped his hand down on the cursed wig.

The cook was a man called Old One Ear. He had lost the other one while a soldier in the Opium War against the long-noses. He was uglier than Old Mao and Red Eye put together, his face pockmarked and twisted and strangely pale, as though he seldom saw the sun. He took Little Pearl around his kitchen and seemed to realize at once that she had never set foot in a high-class kitchen — that the pork for one meal for the Sung family was more meat than she had probably eaten in her lifetime.

"Don't stare at the food," he shouted. "You look like a three-day-old fish."

Wang Lee shook his head in apology.

"Here," the cook said gruffly. "Eat. I can get more work out of you if you aren't half-starved." He set on the counter a steaming bowl of rice covered with a sauce of meat and onions and cabbage, flavored with garlic and red pepper. Wang Lee's nose quivered with pleasure as he shoveled it into his mouth with his chopsticks. "Humph," said One Ear, "you country girls eat like luggage bearers."

Wang Lee swallowed and tried hard to lift his face out of the bowl and take daintier bites, but the smell and taste of the feast compelled him to eat faster and faster. When he pushed his chopsticks around the bowl to capture the last grain of rice, One Ear stuck out his hand. "Here," he said, "one more. But that's the last until tonight, you hear?"

A second helping of this food from Heaven? Wang Lee handed the empty bowl to the cook, who filled it up once more and handed it back. This time the boy was able to force himself to slow down.

"Where is your ancestral home?" One Ear asked. He was chopping a stalk of celery cabbage with a huge cleaver. But he was not watching either the cabbage in his left hand or the cleaver in his right; he was watching his new maid.

"Near Heng Mountain." Wang Lee's mouth was full, and his eyes bulged as he watched the metal flash up and down on the chopping board within an inch of the cook's big fingers.

"That's a long way." The cook still did not bother to watch what he was doing.

Wang Lee nodded and stuck his face into the rice bowl so as not to be called down for making fish eyes again.

"Your father's a fool."

Wang Lee nearly jumped to his feet in anger, but realized in time that his "father" was Red Eye, whose honor he felt no need to defend.

"Only farmer I ever heard of couldn't tell a son from a daughter."

Wang Lee choked on a bit of cabbage and nearly fell off his stool coughing.

The cook put down his cleaver, strolled over, gave a sharp, expert rap between the shoulder blades and then went back to the chopping block. "Don't do yourself in. I won't tell on you. I'd much rather have a bull calf around here than a bawling homesick heifer." He began to chop again, still watching Wang Lee. "You can sleep and bathe in here. Take care you're alone when you relieve yourself in the little house, and Little Pearl should keep her luster for some months to come." He threw the cabbage into a sizzling pan and began to toss it with long cooking chopsticks. "What luck you're so ugly. If you were the least bit attractive, the master or the young masters might take a fancy to you, and then where'd you be?"

Little Pearl proved herself a clever, modest, and very strong kitchen maid. The cook yelled continuously at her just to show how pleased he was. Except for the constant sound of artillery and higher prices, the House of Sung hardly knew that the city was under siege. But suddenly one morning, the guns were silent. What did it mean?

One Ear rushed out to market to get the gossip; there was no question of his sending Little Pearl on a day like this. He loved to be the one to spread the news of fortune or disaster through the women's quarters. He particularly fancied disaster. The women squeaked and bawled so amusingly.

With clouds covering the late November moon, and rain providing a thick curtain around the city walls, the long-haired rebels had crept silently from Miao-kao Hill down to the river where they had bought (some of the cook's informants said stolen) everything afloat from junk to raft. They had gone northward, downstream on the Shiang River. By now they might well be in the lake country of Hunan, almost to that great Son of the Ocean, the Yangtze River itself. They had left no boats behind. The Manchu knew or certainly should know that it would be foolish even to attempt to pursue them.

Wang Lee could hardly keep from weeping. He could see Mei Lin, standing beside her little gray horse on a great flat barge, one arm flung across the horse's neck, her face to the wind. Her ebony hair was glistening with crystal raindrops, her eyes bright, searching the water ahead. How strong and beautiful and wise she was. And now gone — gone to the Yangtze and, from there, on to Nanking where she, a leopard colonel, would be rewarded with position and wealth worthy of all her valor and sacrifice. While he, he was a kitchen maid in an ill-fitting wig, caught behind the walls of a provincial capital. Even if Heaven in its infinite mercy let him look at her face another time before he died, he would never again be close enough to hear her voice or feel her touch. Mei Lin was as removed from him now as Heaven from earth. How had he blundered so thoroughly? He had squandered all the good fortune that Heaven had given him by her hand. First, because he was ignorant; then, because he was arrogant; and last, because he was weak.

He forced his heart to prayer as a gatekeeper pulls and strains at a gate which has stood so long closed that the hinges have rusted shut. He did not pray to be with her. He did not dare risk the wrath of Heaven with such a request, but he did pray for forgiveness and somehow to be allowed to be with his brothers once more — with Chu, dear Chu, who would not condemn. He did not ask for restoration. He would never be a prince or noble or even a leader again. It would be better to be a pigboy in the Heavenly Kingdom than to rule in the Forbidden City of the Manchu emperor. As soon as his hair was long enough, he would escape.

In the meantime, he had made another friend in the House of Sung besides One Ear. She was the little daughter of Sung's second wife. One Ear saved sweets and dumplings for her, and she would skip into the kitchen and climb up on a high stool to eat and be with them while they worked. One Ear would tell Precious Jade tales of Monkey, who stole the peach of immortality and was chased through earth, sea, and sky. And she would clap her hands with delight when Monkey outwitted Heaven and Hell. At first Wang Lee was afraid of her. Suppose the child should find him out? He could not hope that a five-year-old would keep his secret from the household. But he could not fear her long. She was like a butterfly flitting through the kitchen and courtyard. Her padded silk overgarment was bright orange, and she lit up the gray winter days as nothing else could have.

Wang Lee did not know many children's stories, so he made a shuttlecock for her with chicken feathers glued to a piece of wood. He taught her how to kick it behind her back, although she could only manage two or, at the most, three successive kicks, and then she would kick it away, instead of up, and have to chase it. "I'm not good like you," she'd pout. And he would comfort her by saying that if she practiced, she'd become much better than Little Pearl.

He was not prepared. It had not occurred to him. One morning Precious Jade simply did not come to the kitchen, and they could hear instead the anguished screaming from the women's quarters.

One Ear pretended deafness. Wang Lee insisted that he listen, that he turn his ear in that direction. A child was crying. Something terrible had happened. It sounded like Precious Jade, didn't it?

"Oh, that." One Ear shrugged and continued about his business. "They're binding her feet today."

"But they're hurting her!"

"No more than usual."

"She's only a baby."

"The sooner they do it, the more elegant the golden lilies." He slapped Wang Lee's bottom with the flat of his cleaver. "Get to work. You can't waste tears over little girls."

Wang Lee banged the pots he was rinsing to try to shut out the sound of her crying. Nothing helped. A pike driven through his belly couldn't have hurt more. Suddenly it stopped. Both he and One Ear stood still, listening to the silence. "Opium," One

Ear said and began at once to scream at his lazy maid to fetch water from the well instead of lolling about the kitchen like a sick turtle.

From that day, Precious Jade never came running into the kitchen. On a sunny morning Wang Lee would see her sitting in the courtyard where one of the maids had carried her. Sometimes she was crying quietly alone. More often there was a maid with her, trying to teach her embroidery, but Precious Jade would prick her finger and start to cry again.

Early one day when One Ear was at the market, Wang Lee found her alone crying. And he carried her into the kitchen and put her on a stool at the table where he was working. "I'm going to teach you a new game," he said.

She looked up at him. The circles under her eyes were dark as bruises, and her face had grown as pinched as an old woman's.

"I'm going to teach you how to read and write," he whispered.

Her eyes flashed almost like before. "You can't teach me," she said. "You're nothing but a big-footed slave girl."

"Hush," he said. "It's a secret." He took a piece of charcoal from the basket and wrote on the top of the table: *Pao Yu* — Precious Jade. Then he stepped back and looked at it. He sighed. "Perhaps this is too hard for you."

"What's too hard?"

"Your name. But see, the first character is very difficult. Too many strokes. Much too hard for a little girl." He began to wipe it off with the heel of his hand.

"Wait!" She grabbed his wrist. "Don't wipe it off. I can do it. Look!" She took the charcoal and retraced Wang Lee's character awkwardly.

"No." He shook his head. "Let me show you." He took the charcoal and slowly went over the character. "You must make each stroke in the proper order."

"It's no better than embroidery," she complained.

"Oh, yes, it is. But you must be patient."

In two lessons she had mastered her name. Soon, when he would pass her in the courtyard, he could see her writing characters in the air with her fingers, practicing the new words he had taught her in the stolen moments at the kitchen table. The circles remained under her eyes, but she began to smile a little when she saw him.

One day in late December, One Ear came in from the market while Wang Lee was on his hands and knees scrubbing the paving stones of the kitchen floor. The cook thwacked the boy's rear with something he held in his hand, and, when Wang Lee looked up startled, pushed a book toward his face. The boy stood up, wiping his hands on his trousers before reaching for the precious thing. It was the *Three Character Classic* — the first primer for Chinese boys — written in sentences of only three characters each.

"I got copy books and brushes," the cook said gruffly, "and a bit of ink."

"How did you...?"

"Ha!" he said. "This one ear is sharper than a fox's." He snatched the book from Wang Lee's hand. "It's not for free. You have to pay."

"What...?"

"You have to teach me, too."

And so Wang Lee taught them both, beginning with the first three-character sentence: *At birth men are by nature good.*

Despite the pain, Precious Jade forced herself to walk on her newly bound feet. Early in the morning, before the rest of the women's quarters was awake, she came, leaning on a little crutch, hobbling stiff-legged on her heels into the kitchen. Wang Lee or One Ear would lift her up on the stool. They were always ready for her. The breakfast rice was steam-ing, the soup simmering. One Ear would climb up on a stool beside the girl's, and their lesson would begin. Wang Lee stood behind, walking from one to the other, looking over their shoulders, sometimes putting his hand over one of theirs to move the brush properly, even though he himself had never written with a brush — only sticks.

His pupils were quick. Sometimes he would laugh and say, "Soon you will know more than I do. Go slowly. Go slowly, or I won't have anything left to teach you." But he loved their eagerness. The old man raced the little girl, each trying to master a new character before the other. It was better to be a teacher to such as these than to be a king. It would break his heart to leave them, but his hair was growing fast, and his brothers had moved down the Yangtze near the place where the Han and Shunshi rivers join it and the Son of the Ocean widens like the sea.

One Ear woke him in the middle of the night. "It's not safe for you here," he was whispering. "The child's maid followed her this morning."

"But why does it matter?" he asked. "It makes the child happy. There is no law that says a girl may not read or write."

"It's not the pupil. It's the teacher, little fool. The only country girls who can read are long-haired rebels."

He jumped out from under his quilt.

"No," the cook said. "Get your rest. At dawn I'll send you to market. By noon I'll have to tell the master that you have stolen the market money and disappeared. So..."

He left the front gate of the House of Sung with a basket on his arm, empty except for a kerchief with one piece of silver and a few coppers tied in one corner and a razor hidden in the folds. The gatekeeper called a cheery good morning, and Little Pearl bowed back. He was on his way.

## CHAPTER NINETEEN
# FROM CHANGSHA TO NANKING

THE SHAME OF CHANGSHA was left quickly behind. Even Hsiao's death faded in the events that followed. The city of I-Yang surrendered almost immediately, and when the Taiping came to Yochow, sympathizers opened the gates and welcomed them into the city. In Yochow, too, a wealthy merchant provided Yang with a powerful flagship and a variegated fleet of smaller boats, and so they moved, five hundred thousand strong, down the Yangtze River toward the great triple city of Wuhan. The peasants of the river valley brought them food. Their enemies fled before them.

The water was the color of mud and the sky the color of ash. It was a wet, bitter winter in the Yangtze valley, but the Taiping did not know the season. They made their own color and warmth. Sometimes Mei Lin could almost believe that Feng had never died. Her soul was light and clean as it had been in those early days before the first battle. They were nearing the end of their testing. Victory would not be denied them. The horrors and sufferings of the past two years would be washed away in the splendor of the Heavenly Kingdom. Soon there would be Great Peace for all of China.

San-niang, as well, began to regain her spirit. She had the lily-footed women make new clothes for herself and Mei Lin and a new banner for her army. "We shall capture Wuhan before the New Year," she said, "and by spring we shall be in Nanking."

It all seemed quite possible until they came to the place where the Han and Shunshi rivers flow into the Yangtze, and the Son of the Ocean becomes so broad that one cannot see the farther shore. They remembered the old saying about Wuhan: *A bridge can never be built; the river can never be crossed.*

Yang ordered all the boats to the northern shore. There he gathered the commanders and officers together, and told them that the Heavenly Father had descended to earth and revealed to him how the river could be bridged, how the three cities, called together Wuhan, were to be taken. Their task was to obey and demand total obedience from their troops. A journey of a thousand miles begins with one step, and he told them what the first step must be. The main body of the Taiping would take Tortoise Hill, overlooking the city of Hanyang, while he and a select group would work on the revealed plan to capture the three cities.

The strategies that had failed at Changsha miraculously succeeded at Hanyang. The miners dug under the city walls while the foot soldiers marched and sang, and fire arrows rained in upon the city. By the time Hanyang fell, the Eastern King was ready. His cleverest advisers had fashioned exploding devices that could tear open city gates and others that gave off noxious fumes. The blacksmiths had wrought great chains of iron, which they stretched in parallel lines first across the Han River to Hangkow and then, in another path, across the Son of the Ocean itself to Wuchang, the largest of the three cities and the capital of Hupei Province. Between the iron chains, Yang ordered the boats arranged bow to stern. And the terrified Imperialists watched from the shore as the Taiping walked across the water that could not be bridged.

San-niang's horsewomen were sent to clean out the hills around Wuchang. People were fleeing the burning city. Some threw themselves into the Yangtze and East Lake north of the city. Others sought the sanctuary of the hills. The women were to see that no one reached safety. It must be presumed that those who fled from the benevolent protection of the Taiping were enemies, not friends, of the High God.

At first the women killed fleeing Imperial soldiers and militia. But then, before they quite realized it, the bodies through which they shot their arrows were no longer in uniform. The people of Wuchang were dying, but the order could not be disobeyed. In the fever of killing, the women had to close their eyes to the sight of white heads and their ears to the cries of children: "Mercy, sister, mercy!" They did not even know that they themselves had been surrounded until suddenly they heard the whinnies and screams of dying horses and saw the flashes of yellow and crimson as their comrades fell to the earth and tumbled away out of sight down the steep hillsides.

San-niang cried out the order, and they turned their backs to one another and fought their way through the Imperial line. The soldiers were few and frightened, despite themselves, by the ghost women bearing down upon them. San-niang's force quickly subdued them with a fierceness that seemed supernatural indeed.

By late afternoon the hillside was quiet. In the distance could be heard the clang and boom and crack of battle in the city far below. San-niang had the women gather up the bodies of their sisters that had fallen close by. They dug a shallow grave, the best they could manage with sticks and sharp rocks, and laid the bodies gently into it. Far into the night they worked, gathering stones with which to cover the bodies, while San-niang stood guard, her face as hard as the stones they laid down.

When the work was completed, Mei Lin went up to her commander. "What order shall I give?" she asked. San-niang seemed not to hear, so she herself ordered the women to return to camp on the shore of East Lake. She helped San-niang mount her horse and then mounted her own. Still San-niang would not turn her face from the mound of stones. "You must rest," Mei Lin said gently.

"How can I ever rest?" she asked. "These" — she waved her hand at the bodies of soldiers and common people freezing in the winter darkness. "And these" — this time she bowed her head at the stones, shining white in the moonlight. "These, my sisters, were more than life to me. How can I rest?"

And Mei Lin remembered the nearly naked form of a boy lying on the bank of another river. For a moment she thought her heart might burst. But then San-niang clicked her tongue, and her horse turned and began to make its way down the hillside. Mei Lin put aside her own pain to follow her commander.

In retrospect, it was perhaps the greatest victory of the New Age — the bridge a Divine pathway, the explosions God's righteous anger, the poisonous smoke the avenging breath of Heaven. For Mei Lin it was a nightmare that returned to haunt her sleep as long as she lived.

San-niang fell ill without the aid of an herb. But by then the triple cities were secured, and Mei Lin could give full attention to taking care of her.

"It is a strange life for you," San-niang said, trying to moisten her cracked lips with her tongue. "Warrior one day and nursemaid the next. No, not a hireling, a true mother. What would I do without you?"

Again a messenger came from the kings to inquire about the commander's health, and once again a piece of bamboo paper was dropped in the courtyard.

The calligraphy was the same as before, but the poem was different:

> *All night I could not sleep*
> *Because of moonlight on my bed.*
> *I kept on hearing a voice calling:*
> *Out of Nowhere, Nothing answered "yes."*

Again she tucked it quickly into her sash until it could be burned, and hurried into the house.

"Who has come to trouble you?" San-niang asked, propping herself up on her elbow to study Mei Lin's face.

"No trouble, elder sister. Only a messenger from the kings to ask about your health."

"Don't lock away the truth from me, little sister. There is trouble."

"He dropped this on the stones." She brought out the paper and held it out to San-niang.

"You know I can't read," the commander said quickly. "You must read it to me."

"But I cannot," said Mei Lin. "It would not be fitting. It is… it seems to be a love poem."

"Then it's not for me," San-niang lay back on the bed, closing her eyes. "No man sends love poems to a woman who can't read."

There was a whirling inside her chest that rose and filled her throat. No, it could not be. She could not breathe.

"I hope," said San-niang, "your poem is from a handsome young officer."

"No, no."

San-niang lifted herself up at the choked sound. "Who then?"

Mei Lin shook her head dumbly and started to rush from the room, but San-niang called to her. "Don't run from me, little sister. Let me carry your burden. You have always carried mine. Come here to me and tell me his name."

Mei Lin went back and knelt beside the bed. "The calligraphy is that of the Heavenly King," she whispered. And burying her face in the rough cotton of the quilt, she began to weep.

"Ah," said San-niang, putting her hand on the girl's head. "See. The ghost warrior weeps real tears. She is a true woman after all." The commander sat up cross-legged on the bed platform and stroked Mei Lin's hair with her long fingers. "I did not weep for my parents," she said. "Or for my sisters." She sighed deeply. "Or even for my own lost soul. I think sometimes the stories are right: I have become a ghost. And then I look and see you riding by my side, and I am human once more. Can you understand?" Mei Lin nodded under the hand.

"Lay down your heart, little sister. Can men, even if they be kings, take away what the High God, the Creator of All Things, has given?" The hand was withdrawn. "I have sworn by Heaven to keep you from harm." The commander had gotten off the bed and was beginning to put on her outer garments.

Mei Lin looked up in alarm. San-niang was still flushed with fever, but she held up her hand for silence. "The time for weakness is past," she said. "God will give me strength. Now, come, we must order a memorial tablet for our sisters on the hillside."

"But if mourning is forbidden…" How strong the teaching was.

"We'll call it a tablet of celebration."

In less than a week, the Taiping were on the move once more. No flood of the Yangtze had ever been so dreadful. At the border of Hupei and Jiangshi provinces, the Manchu general threw his own body into the Son of the Ocean, but the gods were blind to his sacrifice. The flood could not be stopped. All who could run fled before it. Northward and eastward, down the broad Yangtze the rebels went.

In Peking the Manchu emperor ordered the graves of Hung's and Yang's ancestors to be dug up and destroyed. The bones of their fathers' fathers were scattered, but to no avail. At this time, Yang gathered the army and reminded them of the water buffalo who, looking upon the lowly ant despised it, spit upon it, and cursed its ancestors, and then boasted to the other buffaloes of his insolence. And finally, the beast made the ant the center of his manure pile and lay down to sleep upon the little creature, satisfied that he had destroyed its life and fouled its memory for ten thousand years. But the ant was revived by the very poison of the buffalo's manure, and it rose and stung the beast in his eye and lives forever on the blind side of his enemy, tormenting him continually. Thus the justice of Heaven is done. "And the High God," he said, "has made us powerful who were once weak."

Before the winter was over, the Taiping had captured the capital of Anhwei Province and with it, silver and rice and a hundred cannon. By the curtain of spring they were at the gates of the most ancient capital, the Celestial City of their dreams, Nanking.

Then the High God, who was not made by man but who Himself made all things, descended from Heaven and revealed to Yang that the city would be in the hands of the Taiping before a new moon rose in the sky. And the Heavenly Army sang hymns of praise and turned the mouths of their cannons toward the ancient walls.

The sun rose eleven times upon the battle. While the cannons called out to one another, the Taiping miners dug under the city walls, and the fire arrows of Heaven fell into the city. Before the sun had set for the eleventh time, the hymns of the Heavenly Army could be heard inside the city walls above the moans of the dying. And the High God again descended from Heaven and told Yang that all who had opposed the coming of the Heavenly Kingdom must perish, and every emblem of idolatry be destroyed, for the Kingdom must be purged of all unrighteousness. Thus all the idols were smashed, the temples laid waste, and the porcelain pagoda torn down. No one could count the number of those who died, for it was more than the stars in the sky. And it was said that when the great General San-niang saw all that had been done for the glory of Heaven, she sat down upon the broken stones of the city wall and wept for joy.

## CHAPTER TWENTY
# PILGRIM TO THE CELESTIAL CITY

WANG LEE STOOD on the hill above Wuchang and stared at the mound of stones with its stark memorial tablet to the dead women warriors of the Taiping. Was Mei Lin one of those lying there? How was he to bear this journey if he saw her dead at every battle site along the way? He forced himself to turn from the place and go back down into the city. His few coins were gone, and he must find some way to eat and continue his pilgrimage.

It was a pilgrimage. As a devout Buddhist puts on the white garments of reverence to make obeisance at each sacred place until he comes at last to the great temple, so he, dressed humiliatingly as a peasant woman, followed the Heavenly Army from battle to battle, aiming for the Celestial City. The Taiping might be in Nanking even now. It would take time for word to travel up the Yangtze valley.

There were no boats coming upstream these days, no merchants, no couriers.

There was no food, no place to beg. The temples were in ruins, the great houses in ashes. What was he to do? He had lived too long among the rich. He could no longer wear hunger casually, like a forgotten childhood charm about the neck. It possessed him like a tiger gnawing and scratching within his belly. There was nothing to eat in Wuchang — no chickens, no dogs, no rats. Every face he looked into was as hollow-eyed and desperate as his own. The children who had strength left grabbed his sleeve with bony little fingers and cried, "Pity, sister, pity!" But most were too weak to cry and only stared at him like the dead of his dreams.

He hurried out of the city through what had been the north gate but which now was a gaping hole. The gate itself, a pile of splintered wood and mangled iron, had been pushed into the dry moat by the victorious army. He followed the towpath beside the mighty Yangtze. In time he met others walking in the opposite direction, but he did not question them. They seemed not to see him, their faces filthy with days of travel, their eyes blank like those who have seen too many horrors. He alone was walking toward war.

When he came to a stream that fed the river, he went up a way until he found a shallow place where he could catch fish among the rocks with his hands. He had no flint and iron, so he scraped the fish with a stone, cut them in pieces with his razor, and ate them raw. Some lucky days he found greens to eat that his shrunken belly did not immediately disgorge. But spring was coming. If he could hold out a few weeks longer, there would be bamboo shoots along the riverbank and early cabbage in the fields. Already the sun grew stronger, warming his thin body through the faded blue garments. He slept in short naps during the day and walked at night, reasoning that as long as he kept moving, he could not freeze to death.

He had crossed the border into Anhwei Province, though he did not know it; he only knew that he had seen once more the devastation of a major battle. "Do not go with the river, little sister," an old woman warned him. "The long-hairs have gone that way, and they have no pity." He did not argue, only thanked her and pretended to head eastward. But out of sight, he turned once more toward the river.

One morning he caught crawfish and a water snake to eat, and tied a frog into his kerchief to keep it alive for another meal. Then, more satisfied than he had been for many days, he curled up around his basket and went to sleep in the sun like a lizard on a warm rock.

He was awakened by someone or something tugging at his basket. He grabbed it and jumped to his feet. Before him stood a man, or what once passed for a man — an Imperial deserter to judge from the rags and the rifle pointed at his head.

"Lay down your heart, sister," the man said. "If you are nice to me, I won't hurt you."

"I have nothing to eat," Wang Lee said.

"Liar. There's something in that basket. First, hand it to me. Then loosen your trousers. A man gets hungry in other ways. A girl like you knows that."

He wanted to laugh. In fact, he thought laughter might burst from him like beans from a dry pod, but somehow he held it in. He bowed his ridiculous little wigged head in a humble, womanly posture and said as sweetly as he knew how, "You are right. This miserable person lied. There is a large frog in this basket. If you have something with which to make a fire, I will roast it for you."

The deserter looked first at Wang Lee and then at the basket, which was pulsating with the movements of the angry frog. Back and forth he looked as though fighting to decide which hunger was stronger. The belly won, for he slid his bundle off his back and shoved it toward the boy with one foot, keeping the gun in his right hand trained on the boy's head.

In the bundle were flint and iron, a knife, chopsticks, bowl, and a small cooking pot. Under the rifle's eye, Wang Lee gathered sticks and leaves and made a fire on a flat rock. Then he slit the frog's stomach with one stroke of the knife and emptied the entrails into the cooking pot. "For soup," he explained to his captor as though he were One Ear lecturing the kitchen maid. Then he dismembered the frog and put a fat leg on the end of the knife and began to turn it slowly over the fire. The juices started; he could hear the sizzle as they hit the flames.

The sweet smell of fresh meat roasting rose in the bright noon air.

"Hurry," the man said. Sweat stood out on his unshaven face.

"Soon, soon," Wang Lee chanted soothingly. "It is most delicious when the skin is crisp and the meat tender." He smiled as sweetly as he could. "They call me Little Pearl," he said, "and I have known many soldiers."

The deserter jerked his gun impatiently. "I will eat first," he said, all his lust now centered on the delicately browning flesh at the end of the knife.

"Shall I make soup as well?"

"Later. After you cook all the meat."

"As you say." Wang Lee rose from his haunches and stretched the feast out invitingly. The soldier could not quite reach it. He stepped toward the fire and tugged at the meat with his left hand. It would not come off the knife, and he burned his fingers yanking at it. "Take it off and hand it to me," he commanded angrily.

Wang Lee licked his fingers and thumb against the heat and pulled off the meat. He blew on it to cool it. He passed it under his nose several times. He smiled at it and blew on it again.

"Give it here!" the man shouted, and in his impatience he grabbed for the meat, forgetting, for that one instant, to keep his gun up. Wang Lee jumped, shoved the barrel aside with his shoulder, and jammed the naked knife blade against the man's throat.

"You stinking son of a turtle," he said. "Drop that gun or I'll put your belly on this knife blade and roast you for lunch."

"You're not even a woman." The deserter was whimpering. "You tricked me." He dropped the rifle, but he was still clutching the greasy frog leg in his left hand.

"Give me that meat."

"Pity me," the man said. "I've had nothing to eat for two days."

"Pity?" Wang Lee asked. "You were about to steal my food and violate me." He snatched the meat from the man's hand.

"But you tricked me," the man cried. "I thought you were nothing but a woman." Wang Lee had never felt such fury. He would have plunged the knife into the deserter's belly, but the man fell to his knees and banged his forehead on the stone, sobbing and begging for mercy. Who could soil his hands with such a filthy death?

Wang Lee stole everything the deserter had, leaving him shivering in his loincloth, his thumbs tied together behind his back. The pig would be able to extricate himself eventually, if he stopped blubbering and concentrated on it. Several miles to the north, Wang Lee threw the uniform and the cloth that had made up the deserter's bundle into the river. And then, reluctantly, the rifle as well. There wasn't even a bullet in the gun — the deserter had tricked him, too — and he must not have anything that would make it look as though he himself were an

Imperial deserter. He put the flint and iron, knife, cooking pot, and bowl and chopsticks (which he scrubbed with sand to clean), into his market basket with the uncooked remains of the frog, and started on his journey once more.

There were two ways to Nanking that spring. You could follow the river, as men had done for a thousand years, or you could follow the devastation. He did not know whether the retreating Imperialists or his brothers and sisters had burned the houses and cities and laid waste the fields. It mattered less and less; the suffering was the same.

But the birds chittered among the stands of bamboo at the river's edge. He ate the tender shoots and drank boiled water from the deserter's bowl. One day he found a turtle and put it in his basket, not for food so much as for companionship — but that night he remembered Feng in the demon's bamboo cage and sadly let his little friend go. "Son of a turtle," he muttered as he watched the little creature waddle down the bank. He might not have been so generous except that he knew he was nearing the end of his journey. He had crossed the border into Jiangsu; before the week was out, he would be in Nanking.

He first saw the walls of the Celestial City shimmering in the sun of early summer. From a distance, the new sections could not be distinguished from the old. "God be adored'" The words of praise slipped out unbidden. The city to which he had come was alive. Fields and rice paddies were green outside its walls. Its gates were open and welcoming, and people moved freely in and out. "It is as they promised," he said to himself. "When Nanking became ours, all things were made right."

There was a newly built footbridge across the small river that wound about the city wall, making a natural moat. He joined the crowd jostling across, and smiled and bowed to everyone. These were his sisters and brothers. This was the Celestial City. At the gate he stopped and knocked upon the small door of the gatekeeper's house. An old woman answered.

"Would you help me, Auntie?" he said. "I am seeking for a brother named Chu. He was a charcoal bearer from Kwangsi and is a soldier from before the first battle."

"This white head is a newborn in the Heavenly Kingdom," she said. "But if you go to the military headquarters in the center of the city and ask, they will surely know, little sister."

His hand went to his wig. He was suddenly afraid. At headquarters he might be recognized. He might be on the list of deserters. For once he was grateful to be a woman.

"I have a cousin," he said. "She is a leopard colonel under the great General San-niang. Would you know where they are quartered?"

The woman smiled, showing her toothless brown gums. "Even this stupid person knows where the great San-niang lives," she said and gave him directions that took him through the narrow streets and brought him to the high brick walls of a house which, he knew, had once been owned by a family more rich and powerful than the Sungs of Changsha.

He knocked on the gate. He could hear someone coming, but it seemed to his pounding heart that it took longer than the drinking of a whole cup of tea for the gate to crack open and a small grayish face to appear. "Yes?"

"God be adored, Auntie," he said to the head of the old lady stuck through the crack. She nodded to indicate she'd heard his salute. "Forgive this silly person for disturbing you, but she has come a long way from the south to see her cousin." Again the woman waited silently for him to go on. He was not used to long, polite sentences in his woman's voice, and it made him anxious to have to keep talking to this impassive little face.

"If you would be gracious and tell my cousin, the leopard colonel known as Mei Lin, that her cousin Little Pearl has come up from Hunan…"

"Ah!" The tight gray face broke open like a lotus bloom. "A cousin! Welcome. Welcome." She moved out of the way of the gate and shoved it open with surprising strength. "Welcome. You're just in time for the wedding. She will be so pleased to have family here."

## CHAPTER TWENTY-ONE
# SEED RICE

"IT's HOPELESS. You know it's hopeless," San-niang was saying. "I'm the daughter of a charcoal bearer. I'm too stupid to learn."

"You are not stupid," Mei Lin said fiercely. "You are a general of the Heavenly Army. Don't waste time fretting. We have only today left."

With this San-niang pushed back the heavy carved chair, got up from the black lacquered table where they were studying, and began to pace the room. It was the largest room she had ever been quartered in, but she strode across it faster than Mei Lin could make the strokes of a single character.

Mei Lin poised her brush for a new word. "Lay down your heart, elder sister," she said. "It cannot be helped."

"What if I fall ill?"

Mei Lin shook her head and bent closely over the paper. "Don't harm yourself for nothing."

San-niang stopped pacing and swung about. "Don't call yourself *nothing* to me."

"I don't. I only meant that nothing will help. You heard the message."

"Oh, yes. I heard it. I have heard all the messages. God descended from Heaven and revealed that kings are to have many wives, and that the first new bride of the Heavenly King is by the order of the High God himself...."

"Hush, sister. It can't be helped."

"Suppose I should say that God descended from Heaven and spoke to me? Didn't the Heavenly Elder Brother speak through my blood brother? Why shouldn't God speak through me?"

"Hush. Come sit down. We need to study."

San-niang began to pace again. "I saw a long-nose idol once in Canton. It was carved in wood — the nearly naked body of a man stretched out to die on a crosspiece." She did not remember that Mei Lin had seen that idol as well. "I asked a Jesus people priest what the idol meant, and he told me it was God descended to earth."

"The Heavenly Elder Brother. You know the story."

"No. No. I forget the stories. I only remember that I swore to keep you from harm, and I have failed."

"Shhh. I won't be harmed."

San-niang was staring out the doorway, hardly seeing the lily-footed servant hobbling across the courtyard from the inner moon gate. "Why did our sisters die?" she asked. "Why did I lead them to death?"

"Hush. Hush. It's all right."

"I condemned my brother. Was he worse than I?"

"Hush before you break my heart."

"What do you want?" San-niang demanded, turning toward the little gatewoman now at the doorway.

The woman was not abashed. "The colonel's cousin is here!" She tried to peek around the general, who was filling the doorway, to see Mei Lin. "Your cousin has come all the way from the south in honor of your wedding!"

Mei Lin stood up and came to the doorway. "Please don't keep my cousin waiting at the gate," she said. The woman smiled happily and did her best to hurry back to the main gate.

"What does this mean?" San-niang asked softly.

Mei Lin could only shake her head and wait until the old woman appeared once more, followed by a tall, awkward form in tattered cotton garments with a market basket over its right arm.

"Careful," San-niang said under her breath. "It may be a trick."

By now, however, the cousin was close enough so that Mei Lin could make out the features. But it was impossible. The boy had been dead for months.

"You are very welcome," she said quietly.

The figure fell to its knees and bumped its head to the cobblestones. "God be adored," said a hoarse

Hunanese voice. "This poor person finds the colonel in good health."

Mei Lin stepped quickly out of the doorway and lifted Wang Lee to his feet. He was taller than she remembered, but his face was as thin as a death's-head. "So my cousin has made the long and dangerous journey to be with me as I prepare to leave for another house."

He bowed his head. He was not going to speak again. He couldn't. Mei Lin dismissed the gatekeeper. When they turned to enter the room, San-niang was standing in the doorway smiling. "Present me to your cousin, sister," she said.

They listened to each other's stories, not the elaborate tales of itinerant tellers, but the short coded tales of soldiers who do not have to paint in the horrors for each other. Then the women took him to a small room where there was a tile floor and a yellow porcelain tub filled with warm clean water and, on a stool, trousers and a jacket of softly spun cotton. "Shall I send a woman in to help you bathe?" Mei Lin asked. He looked at her in terror, and then realized that she was teasing. When he was clean and dressed, he returned to their large room where the table was loaded with food. He sat down on one of the carved black chairs, but he could hardly eat. His stomach had lost the habit — or perhaps it was her closeness. She was wearing a fragrance of some kind. He could not place it, but it smelled like a forgotten flower of his childhood — like spring on a mountain.

"You must try to eat a little something," she said. "You are like bamboo." How beautiful she was. There was no turban to cover her lovely, shining hair, and her eyes were dark and shone when she spoke to him.

He wanted to think, poor fool, that looking at him was filling those eyes with light.

San-niang moved in and out of the room, almost like a faithful servant, never allowing anyone else to enter. When it grew dark, she brought in the dish of peanut oil with its faint, sputtering wick. It was like that first night in Kweilin, only then Mei Lin had been a man, and now, at the last, he had become a woman. He began to laugh, and when she asked him why he was laughing, he could not tell her because he couldn't stop laughing. How absurd it had all been. All the time they had spent together. Why had Heaven made him such a fool? He was like a pig wallowing in its own waste.

"You are very tired," she said.

"No," he said, choking on the words. "It's all right. I just remember..." and he was laughing again. The laughter stabbed at his chest and caught in his throat. He could hardly breathe. He might die, and it would be said that the pigboy died laughing. But it wouldn't matter. Tomorrow she would go to the house of the Heavenly King, and he would never see her again.

She was leading him like a child to the bed platform and helping him sit down. She knelt and slipped off his sandals. "Lie down," she said. "Try to rest."

And then, without warning, the laughter turned into sobs, and his whole body shook with weeping. She put her arms around him, as she had once long before, while he covered his eyes like an injured child and wept without shame.

San-niang's voice came from the doorway. "I have told the servants not to disturb the colonel and her cousin," she said. "Tonight you are free. In the morning, you must do as you are told."

When she was gone, Mei Lin undressed him and then herself and drew him to her on the bed and comforted him. He gave himself to her, and it was as though they had plunged into the Son of the Ocean and washed away all the shame and suffering and death of the former days.

When he woke, light was coming into the room through the oiled paper windows, and he was alone. He sat up so quickly that his head spun, not remembering for a moment how he had come to be in a house at all. Then, with a spurt of pain, he realized that she had been with him but was there no longer. Had she left for the King's house as he slept? Before he could curse or mourn, he heard a great commotion in the inner courtyard. He ran to the window and poked a finger through the oiled paper.

Four chair bearers were coming through the moon gate into the courtyard. They were carrying a bridal chair with gilt carvings and red silk curtains embroidered with two dragons and two phoenixes facing the sun. It was the emblem of the Heavenly King.

Then he saw the bride. She was dressed in a long red robe with wide flowing sleeves. The robe had a broad yellow panel that began at the throat and went across her left breast down to the feet and around the hem. There were embroidered borders around the base of the sleeves as well. The embroidery was too delicate to see, but he knew it was the King's sign that bound her, repeated over and over again by the jealous fingers of the lily-footed women. The headdress was high and jeweled, with a veil so heavy that she could not see to walk but had to be led by two young women to where the chair for the King's bride sat waiting. The courtyard was filled with women, smiling, laughing, cheering her. Was she not the most fortunate of all women?

How tall she stood. She moved like a goddess, her head high, despite the weight of the headdress and her own blindness. Too soon she was climbing through the parted curtains, seating herself in the chair. In a moment the curtains would be pulled and fastened, and he would never see her again.

He must see her just once more. No one could deny him that. Just to say good-bye. To say thank you. He rushed to the door, but when he reached out to pull it open, the stock of a gun came out of the shadows and crashed down on his head. "Sorry, brother." There was a shower of jeweled lights, and the cool of the stone against his cheek, and a familiar voice far in the distant darkness saying, "Only use I ever found for this turtle-dirt matchlock."

When he came to, he thought he was suffocating.

He began to claw at whatever was covering his face, falling into his mouth, but someone grabbed his hands. "Keep still. Do what I say." It was Chu's voice. He knew it was Chu. "Stand up, now." He tried. He was slumped in one of the carved chairs, but he stumbled when he tried to get up and had to be helped. "Back off, you're standing on the robe." He could feel his feet now, covered in soft silk shoes with thick cotton soles. He could see nothing through the veil except blurred light, but there was a swish of long silk garment about his legs, and he could feel the embroidered border with his fingertips.

"Whooo." Chu let out a long sigh. "What a job it is to dress a woman." He patted Wang Lee on the back. "The chair is in the courtyard. Not so fancy, only two bearers, but I'm only just a lieutenant. My bride can't expect a lot of ceremony." Wang Lee could hear Chu moving toward the door, opening it an inch or two, closing it back. "After I'm safely out of here, two sisters will come to lead you to the chair. Please, little brother, I beg you, not a sound. Be the most humble of all the virgin brides of China. Not a sound." The door opened and closed.

How long he waited, hardly able to distinguish even the large shape of the bed platform, he did not know. He dared not try to sit or even shift his weight from one foot to the other. At last the door was thrown open. Two giggling shapes came toward him from the lightened area and took him by either hand. "How lucky for cousins to marry on the same day!" said one. "Watch" Don't trip on the threshold!" said the other. They led him out of the room across the courtyard toward the familiar shape of a curtained sedan chair. He was helped to sit down, the curtains pulled, and he was imprisoned in near darkness.

Abruptly, the chair jerked and rose into the air to the grunts of the carriers and the crying of farewells and good wishes and the hope for many children from those who had led him into the yard. Then the bone-jostling ride began. He had had no idea, when he was a bearer, of the discomfort of the rider. He'd always fancied that it was quite a luxury to be borne about in a cushioned chair, but then Chu had obviously gotten the cheapest bearers in Nanking. They ran, but it was the gait of stray dogs, not the smooth coordinated trot of seasoned sedan men.

Out of the main gate of the house they went, into the crowded streets of the city. Where were they taking him? Then he heard the front carrier's "Make way! Make way!" Chu was carrying him himself. There was no need for anxiety. He was bumped and jolted through the narrow streets of Nanking, just as he had carried so many through Changsha. He did not have to see. He could read the smells and sounds and tell what the scene must be. This was the food market. He knew at once from the strong odor of ripening meat, the more friendly smell of fresh greens, the cries of the hawkers. Before too long they had passed out of the city gate into the open country where the strong sweet smell of human fertilizer warmed his nostrils.

The bearers did not stop. On and on they ran. He wanted to call out to them, tell them to rest, or better yet, to let him carry Chu for a while. Chu, after all, was an old man, not used to bearing a sedan chair at a fast jog down a bumpy country road. But Chu had ordered him not to make a sound, so he obeyed and held his peace, li after li, until the ever deepening darkness behind his curtains and veil told him that it was almost night. Then, finally, he heard Chu call the halt. The bearers stopped and put the chair none too gently on the ground, knocking him nearly off the seat.

Chu stuck his twisted face between the curtain. "Forgive our rudeness, my dear bride, but the wedding is over. No more carrying you about like a king. Out you come!"

Wang Lee got out of the chair, so stiff and bruised he could hardly stand, but he managed to straighten and pull off the veil.

"Why she's lovely. What a lucky husband you are!"

In the dusk he could barely make out her face. Her turbaned hair fell about her shoulders, and she had — could it be? — a straggly mustache.

"San-niang was right," said Chu. "No one will look into a bridal chair or behind a mustache."

Mei Lin yanked off the mustache. It had been glued on tightly, and she winced as it pulled the skin. She began to cry softly.

"Don't, little sister," said Chu. "She said — she *commanded* you not to grieve."

"What kind of a man is he?" Mei Lin asked. "What will he do to her?"

"She is a general, beloved of all the people, and a sister of the Western King. Surely he will respect her."

At last Wang Lee understood. The regal bridal chair that came this morning to fetch Mei Lin had instead carried San-niang to the house of the Heavenly King.

The three companions changed into the clothes of common peasants and, in a few more hours, had left the chair and the Celestial City far behind, and turned back toward the Yangtze. San-niang had given Chu money and provisions for their journey, and when they spotted a boat tied up along the bank, he woke the boatman, and paid him well to tow them upstream. At the triple cities they were able to find a small open-decked barge whose owner was willing to take them up the Shiang to Changsha, but they got off before they came to the city and walked the rest of the way to the red earth of eastern Hunan, where the ancestors of Wang Lee still slept in the hillside.

The fields were a tangle of weeds, but the hut stood, and there were ripening persimmons on the tree. He had hoped by some Divine miracle that his parents might be there, that he could, like a proper bridegroom, bring his new bride to his parents' house. But the only life within was the field mouse who scurried away when they entered.

Chu stayed a few days and helped them clean and

repair the hut. With the last of the general's money, he walked to the village and bought a hoe, saddened that he did not have enough left for a plow. It was too late to plant rice for that year, but Wang Lee opened the wall — the fifth brick at the northeast corner — to show them the legacy his father had left. "We will plant in the spring," he said.

Chu would not even stay the winter. He was off to carry charcoal from Thistle Mountain. "I miss the gossip of the journey," he said when they begged him to stay. "But when my old soul needs time to catch up with my body, I'll come back." Before he left, he handed Mei Lin a small, silk-wrapped object. "The general said to give it to you," he said. "She could not wear it to the king's house."

So when it was time to plant the seed rice, there were only the two of them. Wang Lee opened the wall and took out the precious seed. "Wait," Mei Lin said. She got San-niang's parcel and opened it, revealing the strange beads. With the point of a knife she scratched something on the back of the crosspiece and gave it to Wang Lee. He looked to see what she had written. It was the four characters Taiping Tienkuo — Heavenly Kingdom of Great Peace.

He did not understand. "It is a promise," she said, "like the seed rice." And though he still did not truly understand, he sealed it into the hut behind the fifth brick in the northeast wall.

# HUNAN 1864

TEN YEARS HAVE PASSED since we planted the seed rice. Chu comes to see us and laughs that his visits must be lucky, for every time he comes, we have had another child. There are four now, two daughters first, then sons, and a fifth to arrive before the winter. The villagers say that the girls will never find husbands because their feet are unbound and we are teaching them to read.

News does not often reach Hunan from the outside world. Only through Chu do we know of the happenings in Nanking. San-niang is dead these eight years. She took fever after the great purge when the Heavenly King, fearing the growing might of Yang, had him killed and his family and followers with him.

For a while all was quiet. The Manchu and the long-noses went to war again and could not be bothered with the Taiping. But once the long-noses defeated the Manchu emperor, they joined cause with him against us.

And now Nanking has fallen, and all the kings are dead. The land lies wasted. There is no more Heavenly Kingdom. There is no more Great Peace. Some will say that the long-noses despised us as heretics and that is why they allied themselves with the Manchu for our destruction. But we were not destroyed by foreign devils, either Manchu or European. We knew the Heavenly Precepts, but we chose a different path; so the Mandate of Heaven was taken from us.

Today we endure only as a promise sealed in a wall. Someday, perhaps, we shall take root in the earth.

# ACKNOWLEDGMENTS AND PERMISSIONS

THE TAIPING HYMNS, declarations, and precepts included in this book have been paraphrased from various sources.

The translations of classical Chinese poems are from the following sources:

Li Po's "Men Die in the Field," page 144, is translated by A. M. Lonsdale in *Anthology of Chinese Literature, Volume I: From Early Times to the Fourteenth Century*, edited by Cyril Birch and Donald Keene. Copyright © 1965 by Grove Press, Inc. Used by permission of Grove/Atlantic, Inc.

The lines from Wu-ti's "People Hide Their Love," page 209; the lines from Tao Chien's "Returning to the Fields," page 212; and the Tsu-yeh love song on page 236 are all from *Translations from the Chinese*, translated by Arthur Waley, Alfred A. Knopf, Inc., 1941.

I am especially indebted to Professors S. Y. Teng and Vincent Y. C. Shih for their works on the Taiping period, and to Professor John Meskill, who read this manuscript, though any errors of fact that remain are, of course, my own.

My deepest thanks go to my father, G. Raymond Womeldorf, who, of all the nineteenth-century long-noses I have ever known, came closest to thinking and feeling Chinese.